ASSISTED LIVING REVOLUTION

SENIOR CARE REIMAGINED

**ISABELLE GUARINO
& KURT COLEMAN**

Publishing Services provided by Paper Raven Books LLC
Printed in the United States of America
First Printing, 2025

ISBN (Paperback): 978-1-7343153-5-6
ISBN (Hardback): 979-8-9931949-0-5

CONTENTS

CHAPTER 1:
THE SPARK

"The profound impact of pursuing a mission-driven career"

My family's introduction to assisted living was a tumultuous and emotional journey, filled with anxiety, heartbreak, and ultimately, hope. It all began when my grandmother, the matriarch of our family, fell and broke her hip. The doctors delivered the crushing news: she couldn't return home alone. The reality of the situation hit us hard—we had to make swift and crucial decisions about her care.

We embarked on a frantic search for a suitable place for her, visiting numerous facilities. Each visit deepened our despair. The options available were disheartening. The costs were astronomical, with long waiting lists adding to our stress. Worse still, the quality of care was appalling. We toured facilities that were unclean, where the staff seemed indifferent, and the food was unappetizing.

The thought of placing our beloved grandmother in such an environment was unimaginable. We felt a profound sense of helplessness, yet we refused to accept this as the only option for her care.

Determined to find a better solution, we decided to hire an in-home caregiver. This choice, while seemingly ideal, quickly became financially untenable. The cost started at around $27 per hour, and with the need for 24/7 care, our expenses quickly skyrocketed to over $19,000 per month. This was a staggering amount, far beyond what most families could afford. We were at a crossroads, knowing there had to be a better alternative. And if it didn't exist, we were so fully committed that we were prepared to create it.

My father, a seasoned real estate investor with over 30 years of experience, took on the challenge with unwavering resolve. During his exhaustive search, he stumbled upon the concept of Residential Assisted Living (RAL). He discovered a small care home that seemed perfect for my grandmother. It was a modest house tucked away in Phoenix, Arizona. It was unassuming from the outside, but inside, it was a revelation—clean, comfortable, and truly felt like a home. The atmosphere was warm and inviting, a stark contrast to the countless other facilities we had visited.

As my father spoke with the owner, he delved into her story and learned about her journey into the RAL industry. He was intrigued by how she managed to create such a nurturing environment and the details around what it took to run a successful care home. The more he learned, the more a new idea began to take shape in his mind.

He calculated the costs and profits: paying $5,000 a month for my grandmother to live there, with ten other residents, meant the home was generating substantial revenue. His business acumen kicked into high gear, realizing the potential for not only providing exceptional care for seniors but also creating a profitable and sustainable business model. My father's discovery was the beginning of a profound transformation in our lives.

Instead of simply signing my grandmother up to live at this RAL home, my father took a bold step. He approached the owner and asked if she would be willing to sell the business and the real estate to him. To his surprise, she agreed. Despite his limited visits to the home and lack of experience in Residential Assisted Living, he seized the opportunity with enthusiasm. He had a strong background in real estate and, more importantly, a genuine love for seniors. He believed that these qualities would enable him to make a positive impact.

With renewed purpose, he set out to create a new standard in senior care, driven by the belief that our loved ones deserved better. He envisioned Residential Assisted Living homes that prioritized quality of life, personalized care, and a true sense of community. My father's journey was born out of necessity but fueled by love and determination. He committed himself to ensuring that no family would have to endure the heartache and frustration we had faced. This mission became his calling, and he vowed to make a difference in the world of senior care.

To be clear, Residential Assisted Living isn't a concept he invented, but rather an existing industry he saw incredible potential in and decided to highlight. This industry has been around for many years, often nurtured by dedicated individuals who recognize the profound value of offering a supportive environment for the elderly. Interestingly, about 70 percent of these smaller care homes are operated by immigrants, who bring diverse cultural perspectives and a deep sense of community to their work, enriching the lives of their residents in unique ways.

Immersing himself in the world of Residential Assisted Living, my father dedicated himself to learning every detail about the intricacies of providing care, managing staff, and ensuring the well-being of the residents. His real estate expertise helped him navigate the business side, while his passion for seniors drove him to create an even more welcoming environment.

With the intent of moving my grandmother into her new home, my father became the proud owner of an established RAL home called Adagio Gardens. He was thrilled to present this beautiful option to her, knowing she would be cared for in a loving environment. Not only would this move save our family from the exorbitant costs of in-home care, but it also symbolized a new chapter filled with hope and dedication.

Tragically, my grandmother passed away before she could move into Adagio Gardens. And while her loss was incredibly devastating for us all, it also marked the beginning of a beautiful new experience for our family as RAL care home owners. My father fell in love with the industry and started spending more and more time at the care home. He found so much joy and fulfillment in having quality care for the residents, who quickly became like family to him.

Motivated by his passion, my father eventually sold all his other real estate investments to focus solely on Residential Assisted Living. He understood that while he couldn't care for his own mother in this home, he could provide exceptional care for countless other grandmothers and grandfathers who needed it. Overnight, he went from having one mother to caring for ten grandmas and grandpas, each of whom he grew to love deeply.

Over the next eight years, he embarked on a journey filled with trials, triumphs, and invaluable lessons. Without a mentor to guide him or shield him from the inevitable mistakes, he often stumbled, but each misstep became a stepping stone, the opportunity to grow and become better. He learned the intricacies of hiring the right staff, mastering the art of marketing his home, and the delicate task of filling it with residents. Each lesson was hard-won and deeply felt.

At the heart of his endeavor was the vision to create a beautiful environment where seniors could feel truly valued and cared for. Through perseverance and an unwavering commitment, he transformed this facility into a thriving community. This wasn't just a business; it was a sanctuary of warmth and dignity for its residents. The pride he felt in his accomplishments was palpable, a blend of his expertise in real estate and a profound passion for the well-being of seniors.

With his initial success, he quickly expanded, purchasing two additional single-family homes to convert into Residential Assisted Living homes. By the end of his second year in business, he had three care homes under his wing, providing safe havens for 30 seniors. He wasn't just offering care; he was giving families the precious gift of peace of mind, knowing their loved ones were in good hands.

His remarkable journey didn't go unnoticed. Friends from the real estate sector began to inquire about his endeavors. When he shared not just the impressive numbers, but the joy and impact of his work, their curiosity turned into inspiration. This wave of interest led to the founding of the Residential Assisted Living Academy, a training ground for entrepreneurs and investors eager to dive into this transformative industry. Through the RAL

Academy, he shared his knowledge and passion, earning the affectionate title of "The Godfather of Assisted Living."

His passion was infectious. My three siblings and I found ourselves drawn to his mission, and over the years, we joined him, falling in love with the positive impact we were making. Together, we witnessed firsthand the shift from tales of neglect and despair to stories of gratitude and transformation. Investors and entrepreneurs thanked our family for opening their eyes to the potential of RAL homes, and for showing them a path to make a meaningful difference.

Though we still hear countless horror stories of seniors in dire situations, they no longer come from our circle. Our students, armed with the knowledge and passion we impart, create safe, nurturing environments for their residents. Yet there are still many who remain unaware of this incredible opportunity.

Right now, we stand at the precipice of the "silver tsunami," a demographic wave that will demand more thoughtful and compassionate care for our aging population. It's a call to action, a chance to prove that a dedicated group of individuals can indeed make a monumental difference. Our family's journey is a testament to this truth, and we are committed to continuing this legacy, changing lives, and inspiring others to do the same.

Years after establishing a proven blueprint for success in this industry, and building a movement from the ground up with the goal of revolutionizing the Residential Assisted Living industry for the benefit of seniors, sadly, in 2021, my father, Gene Guarino, passed away. He was a courageous and visionary leader. His heart for people and his drive to achieve great things have inspired tens of thousands across the country. His presence has left an indelible mark on so many, and his absence will be felt for years to come.

Thankfully, Gene built an incredible team of experts with huge hearts and a passion to continue the work he began. Carrying on this legacy has been an honor for our family and our RAL Academy team. We've seen firsthand the transformative power of providing a nurturing, homelike environment for seniors. It's not just about offering a place to live; it's about creating a community where every resident feels valued, loved, and supported. Through this journey, we've discovered that true success lies in the ability to make a positive difference in the lives of others, one loving home at a time.

CHAPTER 2:
LOST IN THE LABYRINTH

*"A journey through confusing systems and empty promises
that too often leave families feeling isolated"*

As a Residential Assisted Living home care provider and educator,
I am constantly bombarded with the gut-wrenching stories of
families who, unaware of the alternatives, find themselves trapped
in the grim reality of traditional care options for their elderly loved
ones. The pain of these stories is palpable, and far too often, the
outcomes are tragic.

I hear about caregivers who, with chilling detachment, seem
to have forgotten the very essence of compassion. These are
individuals who should be the guardians of dignity and comfort,
yet their care is often cold and mechanical, lacking the warmth and
understanding that our seniors so desperately need. The higher-ups
in these facilities are also often detached and indifferent, failing to

address the genuine needs of both the elderly residents and their families. The amenities that were once the selling points of their facilities are left unused and forgotten.

Families are often blindsided by exorbitant costs that far exceed what was initially promised, leaving them grappling with financial strain and disillusionment. Instead of addressing the real issues, these facilities resort to alarming shortcuts—double diapering, overmedicating, and outright neglect—trading care for convenience and profit. The reality of it all is deeply disturbing.

It's a betrayal of trust so profound it makes my heart ache. These are our parents, our grandparents, the very people who shaped the world we live in. To see them discarded and treated with such disregard is infuriating and profoundly disheartening. This is not just a flaw in the system; it's a moral outrage, and it should stir a deep sense of outrage in all of us. The system is fundamentally broken, and it's failing countless families who don't even know there are better options out there.

Imagine a grandmother who devoted her entire life to nurturing and guiding her children and grandchildren, pouring every bit of her love into raising them, only to find herself alone in a sterile, impersonal facility in her twilight years. She spent decades creating a warm and loving home, yet now faces an environment that feels cold and alien. It's a stark and heart-wrenching contrast to the life she once knew.

Your destiny should never be to wither away in a sterile institution, where you are reduced to a mere number in a labyrinth of hallways and lifeless rooms. These are places where the warmth of human connection seems like a distant memory, and the care you're paying for feels like a cruel illusion, leaving you neglected just when you need compassion the most.

No, that is not the future you deserve! Your true destiny should be a life surrounded by genuine love and attentive care. Imagine being enveloped by family members and dedicated professionals who not only understand but embrace your evolving needs. These are the people who stand by your side through every triumph and setback, who offer their support without judgment, whether you have a moment of weakness, a lapse in control, or problems with your memory.

This should be the standard of care, a basic right, not a rare exception. It should be the norm that you receive such heartfelt support and understanding, not something that only happens within the comforting walls of your family home.

In-home care, while a noble intention, brings its own set of daunting challenges. The extensive demands of caregiving—those moments of personal care and vulnerability—can be especially challenging for family. When daughters and sons take on the role of full-time caregivers, a choice that is usually made out of love and devotion, it can quickly become an overwhelming burden, straining family connections and leading to resentment and guilt. It's a heavy responsibility, and most family members are not equipped to handle it. These situations can create a sense of helplessness and frustration for both the caregiver and the one receiving care. It is not dignified to wipe your mother's bottom, even if she once wiped yours.

Feeling like you have to drop everything to become a full-time caregiver for a loved one because the common alternative is moving them into a large, hospital-like facility where they're just another number is a horrible scenario. Yet so many people face this very decision every day. The choice is between in-home care, which can stretch family resources thin and test personal relationships, or large, institutional facilities that often feel impersonal and cold. It is a heart-wrenching moment, where the fear of compromising a loved one's well-being against practical constraints weighs heavily. Treating our beloved seniors like this is not okay, and deep down, you know it too.

Thankfully, there is hope. There is a real alternative—a better alternative—an option that blends professional care with a nurturing, homelike environment. Although this option may not be as widely known, this book and my passion are focused on shining a light on these possibilities, and sharing this message of hope with families and everyone who will listen.

The most crucial piece of advice I can offer is to educate yourself before you're faced with the difficult reality of needing to find appropriate senior living accommodations. Don't wait until it's too late for you or your loved ones.

Our mission at RAL Academy is to positively impact 10 million people across the country by promoting high-quality assisted living in residential settings. We're here to guide you toward a better solution, one that honors the dignity and care of our nation's precious seniors.

Imagine the emotional weight lifted when you find a care solution that respects and cherishes your loved one, instead of the common choices that often feel like a last resort. Picture a scenario where seniors are not just receiving the necessary care, but are surrounded by an environment that values their dignity and individuality, without causing undue stress on their families. This is not just a lofty ideal but a tangible reality, a standard of care that should be available to all, not just an exception to the rule. And the good news is that it's happening right now, in small boutique Residential Assisted Living homes dotted all across the country.

Let's not wait until it's too late. Now is the time to start the conversation, to explore and embrace the best possible care options for our beloved seniors. With knowledge and foresight, we can make decisions that honor their dignity and well-being, transforming their later years into a time of comfort and respect.

Residential Assisted Living homes represent a significant portion of the care landscape, accounting for 59 percent of all assisted living beds as of 2024. We are out there, and we are making a difference. RAL homes may not have the flashy marketing budgets of big names like Brookdale, Sunrise, or Atria, but they are driven by something even more powerful: the heartfelt commitment of private owners who invest with their hearts and souls.

Step through the doors of one of these homes, and you'll immediately sense the difference. It's a bit like the first time you used Uber—initially daunting and unfamiliar, but then you discover a whole new level of comfort and ease. You might even find a Residential Assisted Living home right in your neighborhood, one you didn't know existed but is quietly making a significant impact in the community. There's something truly special about community members helping other community members, often in understated, behind-the-scenes ways.

The essence of Residential Assisted Living is not about grand chandeliers, opulent exteriors, or fancy driveways. It's about creating a warm, welcoming environment where comfort and care take preeminence. It's about ensuring that every resident feels valued and at ease. The services and care provided are centered around health, relationships, comfort, and a peaceful transition in the last chapter in one's life. And isn't that what we all want?

Once a person discovers these compassionate options, it becomes impossible to not want to spread the word. Residential Assisted Living homes offer a unique blend of independence and personalized support. With better food, a higher staff-to-resident ratio, and meaningful activities, these homes stand out not for their appearances but for the genuine quality of care they provide. It's a win-win-win scenario, where everyone benefits—residents, their families, and the community as a whole.

Picture a world where the golden years of life are spent in comfort, dignity, and joy. For approximately 70 percent of seniors, this dream necessitates some form of home care and assistance, with the extent of this care varying greatly from one individual to another. As the vast baby boomer generation ages, we face an unprecedented surge in demand for senior housing options that are as diverse and adaptable as the people they serve.

Senior housing cannot be a one-size-fits-all solution. Each senior's journey is unique, and their needs can be complex and varied. Consider those with higher acuity needs, individuals living with dementia, or seniors who may find themselves without an adequate social network. For them, the importance of representation in senior housing cannot be overstated. Equally important are the seniors who cannot afford the exorbitant costs often associated with elder care. For these individuals, access to affordable, high-quality care should no longer be seen as a luxury—it's a necessity.

We must provide a range of options to ensure every senior can find a living situation that suits their unique needs and circumstances. This means creating affordable care options for those on a tight budget, offering specialized care for seniors with specific health conditions, and fostering environments that encourage social connections and engagement.

Residential Assisted Living homes are communities founded on what truly matters—quality of life, comfort, and personalized care. In these communities, seniors are not just residents; they are family. The environment is warm and inviting, the care is compassionate and tailored to each individual, and every day brings opportunities for joy and connection.

For those living with dementia, specialized care can make all the difference, providing a sense of security and routine that helps them thrive. For seniors without a robust social network, these communities offer a built-in family, with neighbors and caregivers who provide companionship and support. For those worried about the cost, affordable options ensure that high-quality care is accessible to everyone, regardless of their financial situation.

By focusing on these elements, we can create Residential Assisted Living communities that truly feel like home. These are places where seniors can enjoy their golden years with dignity, surrounded by people who care. In these communities, every senior's unique needs are met with empathy and respect, ensuring they can live their lives to the fullest. This is the vision we strive to achieve—a world where every senior can find a home that meets their needs, supports their well-being, and nurtures their spirit.

We've all heard the heartbreaking stories—families struggling to find the right care for their aging loved ones, making difficult choices with limited information, or realizing too late the consequences of a decision made under pressure. The inspiration for this book comes from the countless real-life experiences of families navigating the often confusing and emotionally charged world of assisted living.

To bring these challenges to life, we offer the following three scenarios, each illustrating the common pitfalls, tough decisions, and unexpected outcomes that many families face. By sharing these stories, we hope to provide clarity, dispel misconceptions, and help you make informed, thoughtful choices when it matters most.[1]

1: *The stories presented in this book are inspired by real experiences and personal narratives. While the core of each story reflects genuine events, certain details—including names, locations, and specific circumstances—have been altered or fictionalized to protect the privacy of individuals involved and to enhance the narrative. Any resemblance to actual persons, living or dead, or actual events is purely coincidental. The intent of these stories is to entertain and inspire, not to serve as factual accounts.*

CHAPTER 3:
THE BEST INTENTIONS

"The heartache of expecting compassionate support only to be met with neglect and disillusionment"

At 80 years old, Margaret lived alone in a cozy, two-story house that had been a cherished part of her family's history for generations. From the outside, it might not have seemed extraordinary, but to Margaret, it was a treasure trove of memories, a living monument to the years of love and laughter that had taken place within its walls. The house had seen countless family gatherings, celebrations, and quiet moments of contentment. Each room held a story, and each piece of furniture had its own tale to tell. The pictures adorning the walls were not just decorations; they were reminders of a life well-lived, a chronicle of happiness captured in moments frozen in time.

It had been three long years since Margaret lost her husband. His presence still lingered in the air, like a comforting blanket on a chilly winter morning. Sometimes, she swore she could hear the deep, resonant sound of his laughter echoing through the halls. His laughter had always warmed her heart, even on the coldest of days. Now, it was just a memory, but a cherished one, something she held onto with all her might as the years passed.

Margaret's life now was quiet and solitary; she found a certain comfort in her routine. Her children visited when they could, their lives busy and full with their own responsibilities. Those drop-ins were precious to her, moments of joy that punctuated the stillness of her days. Each visit was a reminder of the family she had built, the love that still surrounded her, even if from a distance.

Over the years, Margaret had become fiercely independent. She had a deep-seated fear of being uprooted from her beloved home, the place where she had cultivated a lifetime of memories. The thought of leaving her sanctuary filled her with dread. It wasn't just about moving to an unfamiliar place; it was the idea of leaving behind the essence of her life, the home that held the echoes of her past, the laughter of days gone by. This fear was not just a passing worry; it was a constant concern that she often expressed to her children. She would find herself pleading with them, her voice tinged with desperation, "Please, don't ever put me in a 'home' when I can no longer live alone."

Margaret's plea was a testament to her attachment to the house that was more than a building; it was her life's story, etched into every nook and cranny. It was where she had felt the warmth of her husband's embrace, where she had raised her children, and where she had experienced the full spectrum of life's emotions. For Margaret, leaving this house would be like leaving a part of herself behind, a part she wasn't ready to let go of, even as she faced the realities of aging.

Though age sought to sap her vitality, Margaret refused to surrender easily. She fought back with a fiery determination, vowing never to let time dull her zest for life. Each day, she found joy in life's simple pleasures—tending to her beautiful garden, baking cookies, and losing herself in the sweet nostalgia of the past. Her independence was her pride, a badge of honor that she wore with dignity. Margaret was resolute in her desire not to become a burden to her family. But life has a way of throwing curveballs when we least expect them, challenging even the strongest of wills.

One late afternoon, as the sun bathed her garden in a warm, golden light, Margaret busied herself among her beloved flowers. The air was thick with the scent of roses and freshly turned soil, and the only sounds were the soft rustling of leaves and the distant chirping of birds. She felt at peace, content in her little slice of paradise. As she reached to prune a particularly stubborn branch, her foot caught on an unruly root hidden beneath the foliage. In an instant, she was sent sprawling to the ground.

A sharp cry escaped her lips as an excruciating pain seared through her side, radiating from her hip. The shock of the fall took her breath away, and for a moment, she lay there, stunned, amidst the vibrant blooms she had nurtured with such care. It didn't take long for the reality of her situation to dawn on her with a crushing clarity—her hip was broken and, with it, the fragile independence she had fiercely guarded. The garden, once a haven, now felt like a trap, holding her in a painful embrace.

But Margaret was nothing if not resilient. Gritting her teeth, she summoned the strength born of a lifetime of perseverance. She began to crawl, inch by painful inch, across the garden's soft earth.

The journey was agonizing, each movement sending fresh waves of pain surging through her body. Yet she pushed forward, driven by the desperate need to reach her telephone. With every ounce of determination, she finally made it inside, her trembling hand grasping the phone to dial 911.

The tranquility of the afternoon was shattered by the wail of ambulance sirens. Margaret was swiftly taken from her garden sanctuary to the cold, clinical environment of the hospital. As she was lifted onto a stretcher, she felt a deep sense of loss, knowing that the life she cherished was slipping away into uncertainty.

As soon as she got the call, Judy rushed to the hospital to see her mother. Her siblings David and Heather arrived shortly after. Seeing their once indomitable mother lying frail and in pain was a heartbreaking sight. The woman who had always been a pillar of strength, who had regaled them with stories of her determination and the importance of family, now lay vulnerable before them. They remembered their pact, a promise never to put her into a nursing home, a commitment they had made out of love and respect.

But this situation was dire. The doctor kept a solemn expression on his face as he explained the severity of Margaret's injuries. She would need round-the-clock care and rehabilitation, far beyond what any of them could provide at home. The harsh reality settled heavily over them; they were at a crossroads, facing an impossible choice. The weight of their promise balanced against the fear of causing their mother further suffering hung in the air, thick with emotion. The future was uncertain, and the decisions ahead felt overwhelming. As they looked at their mother, now so fragile, they knew their next steps would change everything.

Over the next few days, the family gathered and spent countless hours fervently discussing their options. They explored every conceivable alternative to institutional care, from in-home caregivers in their mother's beloved home to temporary respite care for her recovery. They knew Margaret would need constant assistance. She could no longer get out of bed unaided, and someone had to be there to tend to her wounds. Over the last few months, the adult children had also noticed subtle changes in her memory, a worrying sign that added another layer to their already complex dilemma.

David, always the pragmatic one, suggested an assisted living facility. He mentioned there was one conveniently located down the street from his home. He believed it would be a good fit for their mother, even though it went against the promise they had made to her. The mere suggestion felt like a betrayal to Judy and Heather, who both immediately dismissed the idea. Heather, the youngest, was quick to explain her situation—she had just received a big promotion at work and didn't have the time or space for their mother in her small home. As the baby of the family, her siblings understood her predicament, though it didn't make the decision any easier.

The burden seemed to fall on Judy's shoulders. At 51, she was at a pivotal moment in her life. Her twin daughters were about to graduate from high school, and she and her husband were on the cusp of an empty nest, a chapter she had eagerly anticipated. The idea of clearing out one of the girls' rooms to make space for her mother crossed her mind, but it came with a host of complications.

Judy worked full-time, her days stretching from 8:45 a.m. to 4:15 p.m., and she cherished the few personal moments she was able to carve out for herself—her weekly wine nights with friends, her commitment to church, and the long-overdue time she hoped to rekindle with her husband. Their relationship had taken a backseat during the demanding years of raising their daughters, and she yearned for the freedom to reconnect and reignite their bond.

The timing of this situation felt like a cruel twist of fate. Just as she was preparing to enjoy a newfound freedom, to rediscover the joys of couplehood, and explore her own interests, this responsibility loomed large. The thought of taking on the full-time care of her mother, with all the emotional and physical demands it entailed, was overwhelming. Judy loved her mother dearly, but the prospect of sacrificing the life she had envisioned for herself and her marriage felt unbearable. The immense weight of the decision was a painful reminder that life's most important choices often don't come with perfect answers. As the discussions continued, the siblings found themselves caught between their deep love for their mother and the difficult realities of obligations and promises to their own young families.

"How about we look into in-home care? Maybe we could hire a caregiver to live with Mom around the clock," Judy suggested, her voice wavering with a mixture of hope and anxiety. "That way, she can stay at home, and we can all try to visit more often. We promised after Dad passed, but... I know I didn't go as much as I intended to." Judy's confession hung heavy in the air. David and Heather averted their eyes, their own guilt clearly just as palpable. Judy knew she had visited their mother far more frequently than her siblings, but even her efforts felt insufficient.

They turned to the doctor for guidance, asking if he had any recommendations for reliable in-home caregivers. He connected them with a reputable agency, and for a moment, it seemed like a glimmer of hope. However, their optimism quickly dimmed as they learned the cost—$27 an hour. For the 24/7 care their mother required, the total came to a staggering $19,440 a month. The siblings exchanged worried glances, knowing there was no way they could afford such an expense, even if they pooled their resources. The option, which had seemed so promising, now felt like a cruel joke.

David, always the problem-solver, suggested they find someone outside the agency, perhaps an independent contractor who might charge less. Judy and Heather reluctantly agreed, hopeful yet wary of their limited knowledge. David took on the task of searching for a caregiver. After several days, he found a woman who seemed ideal. She had worked with three other families, and during their interview, she came across as warm and competent. The cost was more manageable, around $7,000 a month. They all agreed to split the expense and informed the doctor of their decision. Within three days, Margaret was back home, accompanied by her new caregiver, and the family breathed a momentary sigh of relief.

Initially, everything appeared to be going well. Margaret was home, receiving the care she needed, and over the phone, things seemed fine. Yet the siblings couldn't shake their concern about her memory lapses. Judy, ever the cautious one, began visiting more frequently after work, dropping by unannounced a couple of times a week. As time passed, her unease grew. She noticed that her mother's medication seemed to be running out too quickly, raising red flags. Then, one day, she spotted a faint bruise on Margaret's right wrist. When Judy questioned the caregiver, the woman explained that Margaret had nearly fallen, and she had to grab her to prevent a more serious accident. The explanation seemed plausible enough, but the unease in Judy's stomach only deepened.

Determined to get to the bottom of things, Judy continued her impromptu visits. The more time she spent at the house, the more worried she became. Little things began to add up—Margaret seemed more confused than usual, the house wasn't as tidy as it had been before, and the caregiver's explanations felt increasingly shaky. The sense of something being "off" gnawed at her, a silent alarm she couldn't ignore. Judy's worry for her mother grew, and with it, the painful realization that their attempt to honor their promise and keep their mother safe at home might not be working out as planned.

One afternoon, as Judy arrived at her mother's house, she was greeted by the sound of Margaret's frantic screams echoing from the bedroom. Her heart raced as she sprinted down the hallway, fearing the worst. She burst into the room and found Margaret struggling to sit up in bed, her face twisted in discomfort and distress. The caregiver, Rachel, was nowhere in sight. Judy rushed to her mother's side, and noticed that Margaret had wet the bed. "Mom, are you okay? Where's Rachel?" Judy asked, trying to mask her rising panic.

Margaret shrugged, her face pale and weary. "I think I've been screaming for her for about 40 minutes now," she replied, her voice a mixture of exasperation and confusion. "Maybe even longer. Two episodes of *Yellowstone* have passed since I needed to get up to pee."

Judy's heart sank. The realization hit her hard: her mother's sense of time and reality was slipping more quickly than they had realized. The situation was becoming severe. She helped Margaret out of bed, guiding her gently to the bathroom. As she cleaned up the bed and changed the sheets, her mind raced with worry and anger.

Nearly 20 minutes later, Rachel finally appeared, reeking of marijuana, her eyes bloodshot and unfocused. The sight of her was a punch to the gut. Judy's fury flared. She locked eyes with Rachel, her voice cold and steady. "Get out of here now. You're fired."

Rachel looked down, clearly embarrassed, and muttered an apology. She asked if she could collect her belongings, and Judy, barely containing her anger, nodded curtly, urging her to hurry. As Rachel left the house, Judy felt a wave of relief wash over her, but it was quickly replaced by a deep sense of helplessness.

Judy turned to Margaret, her voice softening with regret. "Mom, I am so sorry. We thought this would be a good solution, but I don't know what to do anymore. I don't think you can stay here alone. Why don't you come home with me?"

Margaret, looking defeated, simply nodded. Judy began packing up her mother's things, trying to ignore the tightness in her chest. But then she noticed something alarming: all of Margaret's pills were missing. She clenched her fists, a fresh wave of anger surging through her. "Rachel," she muttered under her breath, feeling a mixture of betrayal and frustration. The caregiver they had trusted was not only incompetent but possibly dangerous. She had been right to mistrust Rachel, but that was little comfort now. As she helped Margaret gather her belongings, she knew they were back to square one, facing the daunting task of finding a safe, comfortable solution for her mother's care.

Judy brought her mother back to her home, bracing herself for the difficult conversation ahead. She sat down with her twin daughters and explained that, for the next few months, they would need to share a room until they left for college. The announcement did not go over well. The twins erupted with irritation, their voices rising in a storm of protests and slammed doors. Their teenage angst created an atmosphere thick with tension.

Judy's husband, Robert, walked into the noisy chaos after a long day at work. He found Margaret sitting quietly in the living room, Judy drenched in sweat, desperately trying to rearrange the girls' room, and the twins' shouts reverberating through the house. The scene was overwhelming, a cacophony of emotions and turmoil. It was as if he had walked into the middle of a war zone. Judy greeted him with a weary sigh, planting a kiss on his cheek. "I'll explain later," she murmured, her voice laden with exhaustion and a hint of desperation. She finally got Margaret settled into the freshly organized room and then retreated to the kitchen, hoping to find some semblance of normalcy in preparing dinner.

Just as she began to chop vegetables, her phone rang. It was David, his voice seething with anger. "JUDYYYYY! Why did you fire Rachel?! I just got a call from her, and she was crying and upset. What did you do?!" His words were a barrage of accusations, each one striking her like a blow.

The pressure in Judy's mind was mounting, her emotions teetering on the edge. Her voice quivered as she recounted the events of the day: finding Margaret screaming for help, the wet bed, the alarming absence of the caregiver, and finally, Rachel's drug-impaired state and the missing medication. As she spoke, tears welled up, her frustration and fear spilling over. "David, she was neglecting our mother," Judy said, her voice breaking. "She was high when I got there, and Mom had been calling for her for over an hour! I couldn't just leave her there. I had no choice."

David's anger began to wane as the gravity of the situation sank in. Judy took a deep breath, trying to compose herself. "I'll be Mom's caregiver for now," she declared, with a mix of determination and desperation in her voice. "I'll talk to my boss and see if I can work from home. Maybe we can go back to the agency and find a legitimate caregiver, someone part-time who can come and go. It won't be easy, but I'll figure it out." She paused, wiping away a stray tear. "I wanted to go to nursing school at one point, remember? How hard can it be to care for my own mother? She took care of me all my life; it's the least I can do for her."

As Judy hung up the phone, she felt the weight of her decision settling on her shoulders. The path ahead was uncertain, and she knew it would be filled with challenges she had yet to anticipate, but her mother's safety outweighed them all. As she stood in her kitchen, surrounded by the familiar sounds of family life, she steeled herself for what lay ahead. Margaret was her mother, and Judy knew that whatever it took, she would find a way to return the love and care her mother had shown her. It wouldn't be easy, but she knew it was the right choice, whatever it cost.

The siblings discussed this new arrangement and agreed. They decided to hire a part-time caregiver to assist Judy during peak hours until they could establish a more stable routine. After long, heartfelt conversations with Robert and their daughters, Judy found herself surprisingly excited about having her mother stay with them. The thought of caring for her mother filled her with a deep sense of honor and pride. She felt privileged to step up and offer her support in such a meaningful way.

The next morning, David sent over some recommendations for caregivers from the agency. The three siblings scheduled Zoom interviews with two candidates, and were particularly taken with the second, a woman named Esmeralda from Guatemala. Her warm demeanor and extensive experience reassured them. They decided she would come to Judy's house from 9 a.m. to 2 p.m., providing care and companionship for Margaret. The arrangement would cost the siblings about $4,500 per month, but it would allow Judy to maintain a shortened work schedule and manage her errands.

Esmeralda began the following week. Judy adjusted her work hours, grateful that her boss was accommodating, though it did mean a pay cut—an unwelcome change just as the girls were about to head off to college. Despite the financial strain, Judy was resolute. This was what she needed to do for her mother, and she was determined to make it work.

One evening, Judy sat down with her daughters to discuss the situation. She spoke with heartfelt sincerity about the blessing of having their grandmother close by, sharing stories of Margaret's strength and the love she had always given. The girls, initially resistant and caught up in their teenage worlds, gradually softened. They reluctantly agreed to share a room until August, when they would leave for school. Judy sensed a subtle shift in their attitude, a glimmer of understanding and acceptance.

Robert was also supportive of Margaret moving in, even though it meant further postponing the couple's long-awaited time together. He understood the gravity of the situation; his parents had passed away in nursing homes, a decision he regretted deeply. Though he was disappointed about Judy's pay cut and the added financial burden, he accepted the challenge. With both girls heading to college soon, the pressure to provide was already high, but Robert believed they could manage.

As the household settled into a new rhythm, there was a sense of purpose and unity despite the hardships. Judy felt a profound sense of fulfillment, knowing she was doing the right thing. There were sacrifices and adjustments, but they were all navigating this new chapter together, bound by love and an even deeper commitment to caring for one another.

Over the next few months, Judy's life began to unravel in ways she hadn't anticipated. Her once-cherished Sunday mornings at church became a distant memory, replaced by the responsibilities of caring for her ailing mother. Margaret's health made it nearly impossible for her to attend services. Getting dressed, navigating to the car, and sitting through the two-hour service were too taxing. As a result, Judy found herself spiritually adrift, missing the connection with her faith community and feeling a growing distance from her spirituality.

The sacrifices mounted. She missed her twins' cheerleading competition, a significant event she had been looking forward to, because Esmeralda, the caregiver, was sick and unable to cover her shift. Although Esmeralda was dedicated and kind, her schedule was rigid due to her commitments with other families, and when she fell ill, there was no backup. Judy's daughters were furious; their cold silence lasted more than a week. The sting of their disappointment cut deep, leaving Judy heartbroken.

At home, Robert grew more distant, his conversations became dominated by concerns over mounting bills. The household expenses had noticeably increased—extra food, higher utility bills, and even an unexpected rise in the cable bill due to Margaret's fondness for renting movies. The financial strain was significant, exacerbating the tension between them. Robert's focus on their tight budget felt like a wall, preventing any meaningful connection.

Meanwhile, Heather had become a ghost in their lives. Swamped with work, she hadn't visited since Margaret moved in, leaving Judy to shoulder the burden alone. Judy's resentment toward her sister simmered, fueled by Heather's absence and lack of support.

David's decision to withdraw his financial contributions was the final blow. What was once a manageable $4,500 a month split three ways now often fell squarely on Judy's shoulders. The financial and emotional strain was overwhelming, leaving Judy isolated and abandoned. She hadn't had a "wine night" with her friends in what felt like ages, cutting off a vital lifeline of social support and companionship.

Physically, Judy was crumbling. The constant lifting of her mother—moving her in and out of bed, chairs, and the bathroom—was taking a toll on her body. Her back throbbed with pain, a relentless reminder of the physical and metaphorical weight she was having to carry. The physical strain mirrored her emotional exhaustion; she felt like an unappreciated caregiver rather than a loving daughter. The resentment she harbored towards her siblings, her husband, and even her mother grew each day. The love and duty that once motivated her now felt like an enormous chain, dragging her down into a pit of anger and frustration.

Judy was falling apart at the seams. Her world, once filled with purpose and love, now seemed small and suffocating. The isolation and lack of appreciation weighed heavily on her, draining her spirit. She longed for a break, for a moment to breathe, but it felt like a luxury she could no longer afford. Every day, the pressure mounted, and Judy feared that one day soon, it would all come crashing down.

Why did it all have to fall on her? Why was she always the one bearing the burden of responsibility? The questions tormented Judy, especially on nights like this one. Her mother's memory was deteriorating rapidly, and it had reached a point where she barely recognized her own daughter. One night, as Judy gently tried to help her mother to the bathroom, Margaret lashed out in fear or confusion, striking her. Judy was stunned, the pain of the slap echoing the emotional pain she felt. That night, she nearly broke. The pressure, the exhaustion, the relentless demands—it was all too much. She found herself questioning everything: why had she agreed to this? Was this truly what being a good daughter meant—cleaning her mother's private areas, sacrificing her marriage, her faith, her time with her daughters and friends? The reality was far from the sweet, rosy image of caregiving she had imagined. Instead of gratitude, her mother offered no thanks, no affectionate kisses on the cheek. The woman who once smelled of roses from the garden now seemed a shadow of herself, and Judy's love was being swallowed by bitterness.

As the years passed, Margaret's health continued to decline. The cost of Esmeralda's care rose by about $500 a month, each year, adding to the financial strain. Robert had become a ghost in their marriage, retreating into silence and distance. Their daughters, now off at college, seldom visited. The house felt emptier without their laughter, and Judy missed them dearly. Her siblings only added to her misery. Heather constantly criticized her caregiving, insisting on an impossible diet of organic and gluten-free food for their mother. When Judy explained that it was financially unfeasible, Heather's biting retort cut deep, "It's like you're choosing to kill Mom slowly. Wow, sister, wow." Judy had grown numb to the hurtful comments, to the persistent guilt, and the feeling of being utterly unappreciated.

David was no better. Caught in the throes of his own divorce, his contributions ceased altogether, and he barely visited, showing up maybe four times a year. Judy felt abandoned by her siblings, their lack of support a constant reminder that she was alone in this overwhelming responsibility. No matter what she did, it seemed like she could never do enough. The constant criticisms, indifference to her sacrifices, the unending financial burdens—all of it made her feel like she was failing. The weight of it all was unbearable.

Judy's resentment grew, not just toward her siblings, but toward everyone around her, even her mother. The resentment was a dark, creeping presence in her heart, staining the love she once felt. The woman who had once been her pillar of strength, her mother, was now the source of her deepest anguish. Judy hated herself for feeling this way, but she couldn't deny the growing anger and frustration. It was as if the light had gone out of her life, leaving her trapped in a relentless, unending darkness.

Judy had given her mother a small brass bell, a quaint object meant to summon her when needed. But each time she heard the bell's sharp ding, like a Pavlovian response, a wave of fury welled up inside her. It wasn't just the bell, or even her mother—it was everything. Judy found herself on the verge of blaming her mother for every burden in her life. The happy, relaxed moments she'd dreamed of for this stage of life were slipping away, overshadowed by a crumbling marriage. Just when she thought things couldn't get worse, RING, her thoughts were interrupted. Her siblings, useless and distant, offered no support. RING! Her daughters seemed devoid of empathy, their faces cold and unfeeling. RING!

She hadn't seen her friends in what felt like an eternity. RING! It was all too much.

Her frustration came to a crescendo when, in a moment, something inside her just snapped. Judy's patience, already hanging by a thread, finally gave way. "I CAN'T HELP YOU RIGHT NOW!!! I NEED A BREAK!" she screamed, her voice raw with distress and exhaustion. She slammed her coffee mug down, the ceramic clanging angrily on the counter. Grabbing her keys, she fled the house, as the door slammed behind her with a resounding thud.

Guilt and a storm of emotions churned inside her—depression, anger, resentment, frustration, abandonment, loneliness, fear. It was just too overwhelming. She drove aimlessly, her vision blurred by unshed tears, until she found herself outside her best friend Kelly's house. Parked in front, Judy couldn't hold it in any longer. The sobs came, heavy and uncontrollable, as she cried and cried into the steering wheel.

After a few minutes, she felt a gentle tap on the window. Kelly stood outside, her face etched with concern. She motioned for Judy to unlock the doors, and when she did, Kelly slid into the car and wrapped her arms around her friend. Judy clung to her so tightly, the tears flowing freely now, her sobs reverberating in the enclosed space. She hadn't realized how much she needed this, how desperately she craved the comfort of someone who understood. Kelly held her firmly, her presence a soothing balm to Judy's battered soul. In that embrace, Judy felt a sigh of temporary relief, and for a moment, the tremendous weight of her burdens seemed to lighten by a few pounds. For the first time in months, she felt like she wasn't entirely alone.

Judy poured her heart out to Kelly, recounting every painful detail. She felt shattered, like a vase that had been knocked off a shelf and scattered into a thousand pieces. The trauma and hurt had built up to an unbearable point, and she had nowhere else to turn. Though she had long abandoned the comforting rituals of wine nights and lengthy phone calls with Kelly, her friend instinctively knew Judy needed her now more than ever. Kelly listened with a compassionate ear, her face full of empathy.

After a long silence, Kelly spoke softly. "I wish you had come to me sooner." She went on to share something that sparked a flicker of hope in Judy's heart. Kelly's father was living in a local Residential Assisted Living home, a place that felt like a haven rather than a cold, sterile nursing home. It cost about $4,750 a month, but Kelly assured Judy that it was worth every penny. The caregivers were so incredibly loving and kind, genuinely getting to know her father like a family member and treating him with the dignity and respect he deserved. Kelly received constant updates and felt secure knowing her dad was happy. He had daily activities that kept him engaged without being overwhelmed, and he enjoyed the comfort of his own private bedroom and bathroom. It was truly the best of both worlds—professional care in an actual home setting, not just a "homelike" imitation.

Judy listened, amazed that she had never heard of such a place. How had she missed this option, something that could have made life so much more manageable? Kelly explained that the owner only had three of these homes in town, each accommodating just 12 residents. They didn't advertise much, relying mostly on word of mouth and placement agents. Kelly confessed she couldn't quit her job to care for her father full-time, so this had been the perfect solution. Her dad was thriving there, happier than he had been in many years.

As Kelly described the home, Judy began to imagine a different life. What if her mother could live in a place like that? What if she could finally step back from the exhausting role of caregiver, a role that had forced her to do things she never imagined, like bathing her own mother? Maybe, just maybe, this could be the key to healing the rift in her marriage. She could reclaim her identity, perhaps even become an empty nester in a real sense, and spend much-needed time with Robert. The thought of working more hours and contributing financially was also a relief, offering a sense of purpose and normalcy she craved.

Judy felt a flicker of hope and thanked Kelly, not just for the invaluable information but for the emotional support she had desperately needed. They agreed that they should revive their wine nights soon, even if they weren't sure exactly when. Kelly smiled, a gentle reminder of the strength of their friendship. She said, "Honey, it's an incredible honor to care for your mom, but I know it's not easy. I would have done it too, but I am just not cut out for caregiving. If it were me, my dad wouldn't have lasted a week under my care! You'll find the right solution for you and your family—I just know it."

With one final hug, Judy left Kelly's house, a mix of emotions swirling inside her. She felt a sense of relief and possibility, holding onto the belief that there might be a way out of the darkness. As she drove home, she embraced the idea that things could get better, that she could find a way to be a daughter again, rather than just an unappreciated caregiver.

As Judy stepped through the front door, the persistent ringing of the bell greeted her. RING RING RING. She sighed and rolled her eyes but headed towards her mother Margaret with a slightly lighter weight. The Alzheimer's had progressed to the point where Margaret no longer recognized Judy, neither her face nor her name. Each time Judy entered the room, her mother looked at her with alarm, as if she were a stranger intruding into her world. Judy had endured years of being cursed at, hit, and kicked by this woman who no longer resembled the mother she once knew. Margaret's confusion was so deep that she might as well have been a stranger herself. This was not the vibrant, independent woman Judy had grown up with—the one who loved gardening, who had a contagious laugh, who used to cook the most delicious pot roast. It was heartbreaking.

But amidst the despair, maybe there was hope with this… "Residential Assisted Living." How had she never heard of this before!? Excited by the prospect of finding a better solution for her mother's care and a chance to reclaim her own life, she began researching options nearby. To her surprise and relief, she found a facility just five minutes away. She scheduled a visit, and was filled with a mix of hope and anticipation. Perhaps there was a chance to restore some normalcy, to bring her family back together.

However, before that hope could be realized, tragedy struck. One morning, Judy went to check on her mother and found her lying still, her skin a ghostly white. Immediately, her heart shattered. Despite all the abuse, the forgotten memories, and the sacrifices she had made, the pain of losing her mother was indescribable. Margaret had been the one who showered her with love, filled their home with the aroma of home-cooked meals, and made the holidays magical. And now, after turning her entire life upside down and caring for her daily for four years… she was gone.

Judy called 911, her voice trembling as she explained the situation. The ambulance arrived, and they took Margaret away. She then made the dreaded calls to her siblings, informing them that their mother had passed away. Despite the resentment Judy felt towards them for leaving the burden of caregiving on her shoulders, none of that mattered in this moment. The harsh reality set in—they were now parentless. As much as Judy had struggled with her siblings over the years, as much as she had resented them, all of those grievances faded in the face of their shared grief. Their beloved mother was gone, and all they had left was each other.

Over the next few months, the siblings' relationship began to slowly mend. Despite this progress, Judy couldn't completely shake the feelings of abandonment that had haunted her during the most challenging time of her life. The bitterness of being left to shoulder the burden of caregiving alone lingered in her heart, a wound that healing couldn't completely erase.

As time passed, her daughters' lives took new turns. Both graduated from college, marking a bittersweet transition. One moved back home to save money before finding her own place, while the other took a job in a distant city. Their relationships, strained by the chaos of the past few years, started to heal. Judy prioritized reconnecting with them, setting aside time each week for long phone calls and heartfelt conversations. Gradually, the emotional distance between them narrowed, and her daughters began to come back into her life, rekindling the bond they once shared.

Judy threw herself into her work with renewed vigor, taking on more hours than ever before. She felt a deep need to make up for the years Robert had carried the financial weight of the family alone. The return to a structured work schedule brought back a sense of independence she had missed dearly. Amidst the hustle, she found solace in church, where she could finally release her pent-up emotions. Sitting in the pews, tears streaming down her face, she felt an overwhelming sense of relief and joy to be back in the presence of the Almighty. It was a place of refuge and comfort, a space where she could pour out her heart and feel heard.

Determined to revive her social life, Judy reached out to her girlfriends and planned a long-overdue wine night. After everything she'd been through, she felt she deserved a little more than just wine—perhaps a strong shot of tequila would be fitting. But the important thing was she was reclaiming her life. She felt a glimmer of her old self emerging from the shadows of grief and hardship.

In the midst of this newfound energy, Judy and Robert began attending couples counseling. Judy was desperate to be the wife he had fallen in love with, but life had repeatedly pulled her away from him. The promise she had made to put him first felt distant, a commitment lost in the shuffle of life's chaos. During one session, Robert admitted that he wanted a divorce but was willing to try working through their issues if she wanted to do the same. The revelation hit Judy hard, but she begged him for a chance to make things right. He agreed, and together they worked on a plan to save their marriage.

Over the next six months, a sense of normalcy returned to Judy's life, maybe even more than before. She reestablished her routines, reconnected with loved ones, and found joy in simple pleasures again. But beneath the surface, the scars from her experience with her mother ran deep. It was almost like PTSD, the trauma of those caregiving years inscribed on her soul. Yet she was back—stronger, wiser, and more resilient. The path ahead wasn't easy, but she faced it with a newfound strength and determination.

Although Judy took great pride in honoring her promise to never place her mother in a "home" or "facility," the reality of caregiving came at such an immense cost. She hadn't anticipated the magnitude of sacrifices required—sacrifices that went far beyond physical care. The emotional and psychological toll nearly broke her. She found herself neglecting the promises she had made to herself, her family, her husband, and her career. The burden of caregiving became all-consuming, and she nearly lost everything she held dear.

In the quiet moments of reflection, Judy often questioned whether it had all been worth it. She would say, "Maybe if I didn't have a husband, kids, a job, and a life of my own... and of course, if I had endless income to afford full-time, in-home care, then it might have been a great option. But I didn't have those luxuries. Doing it all on my own almost killed me."

Judy regretted not fully researching all the care options available. She realized far too late that many of her decisions had been driven by emotion rather than logic, made hastily in moments of desperation and fear. The result was devastating. Instead of preserving the dignity and bond she once had with her mother, Judy felt she had lost her entirely. The roles had reversed so completely that the loving mother she remembered was overshadowed by a figure she barely recognized—a woman who no longer had the strength to be kind or the capacity to remember who Judy was.

"It wasn't dignified," Judy confessed. "A child should never have to wipe their mother's private areas, bathe them, or be subjected to verbal and physical abuse from someone they love."

These tasks stripped away the remnants of their relationship, replacing affection with resentment. The woman who had once been her loving mother turned into someone she dreaded seeing, a source of constant anxiety and emotional pain. The caregiving experience became a nightmare, turning her cherished memories into a haunting alternate reality. She felt trapped, with no one to turn to and nowhere to escape the relentless demands.

KEY TAKEAWAYS

Judy's experience serves as a cautionary tale. While the idea of caring for a loved one at home may seem ideal, the practicalities can be overwhelming. The level of care required, the progression of a loved one's needs, and the caregiver's personal circumstances can make this seemingly noble choice a path to emotional and physical exhaustion. It can strain relationships, erode personal well-being, and transform love into resentment. The parent Judy once adored became a source of anger and bitterness. The harsh reality is that caregiving without adequate support and resources can lead to feelings of isolation and deep regret.

Judy's story is a powerful reminder that sometimes the best intentions need to be balanced with realistic assessments of one's own capabilities and limitations. It's crucial to explore all available options and consider professional help, not only for the well-being of the aging loved one, but also for the caregiver's own mental and emotional health. Caregiving is an act of love, but it should not come at the cost of one's own life and well-being.

CHAPTER 4:
SHATTERED EXPECTATIONS

*"The painful disconnect between the advertised
promise and the harsh reality of care"*

The Harrison family had always regarded Christmas Eve at Dad's house as a sacred tradition. Each precious family memory was intertwined like the roots of a sturdy tree, anchoring generations together. It was an unspoken rule that no matter where the winds of life scattered them, they would always return home for the holidays. For Jason, Bob, Thomas, and George, these snowy December evenings weren't just a holiday ritual; they were a pilgrimage to the heart of their family. Over the years, this tradition had grown even richer, as their children joined the gathering, bringing a new sense of wonder and excitement that rekindled the joy they remembered from their own childhoods.

As he drove, Bob's mind wandered, harkening back to those perfect, beautiful snapshots of home, and being surrounded by the people that he cherished most. Each year, the approach to the family home felt like stepping into the enduring comfort of a storybook Christmas scene. Though the house was nestled in a blanket of pristine snow, it exuded warmth and welcome. As the front door swung open, a soothing heat from the roaring fireplace enveloped them, chasing away winter's cold bite. The air was sweet with the fragrant aroma of sugar cookies baking in the oven. It was a smell that instantly brought back memories of laughter and sticky fingers from frosting sessions around the kitchen table.

The Christmas tree, standing tall and proud in the living room, was a testament of the family's rich memoirs. At twelve feet, it towered over the room, a beacon of light and color. Its branches were laden with ornaments, each one a precious relic from Christmases past. There were delicate glass baubles from their parents' early years, as well as handmade crafts from when the siblings were young. And now, there were new additions from the grandchildren, who delighted in seeing their creations take a place of honor. The tree was more than decoration; it was a living tapestry of the family's shared history and love.

In the background, the soft crooning of 1950s Christmas classics added a nostalgic soundtrack to the scene. The familiar melodies had played every year for as long as the brothers could remember, each note a comforting reminder of tradition. In the kitchen, Mom and Dad made the final preparations for the feast with an ease that spoke of decades spent perfecting their holiday customs. They moved together like a well-rehearsed dance, exchanging smiles and quiet words as they checked on the roast, mashed the potatoes, and stirred the gravy. The sight of them working side by side was the heart of the family's Christmas, and their love was evident in every gesture.

The wistful memories of holidays past began to fade as Bob's wandering mind came back to the present. Turning the familiar corner into the neighborhood, a knot of dread tightened in his chest. This year was going to feel unlike any before, and a heavy cloud of sorrow hung over the family. His wife reached over and gently squeezed his hand to offer her silent support. The children sat quietly in the back, uncharacteristically subdued. The loss of his mother, just two months prior, had cast a long shadow over the family. Her absence was a cavernous hole in their lives, a wound still raw and aching. The thought of entering that house without her there, without her endearing laughter, without her warm inviting smile, it was unimaginable.

As the car approached the driveway, the stark reality of the change hit Bob with a cold, jarring clarity. The house stood silent and dark, a bleak contrast to the usual festive cheer. There were no twinkling lights adorning the roof, no cheerful decorations heralding the holiday season. The front yard, usually meticulously shoveled and decorated with a snowman and festive displays, lay untouched, the snow deep and undisturbed. It was as if the house itself was in mourning, reflecting the family's grief.

Bob parked the car and tried to take a deep breath, but the tension felt like a knot forming in his heart. One of his children, their voice trembling with emotion, broke the silence. "Dad, I really miss Grandma. Do we have to go in?" The words hung heavy in the air. Bob felt a lump rise in his throat, his own grief mirrored in his child's eyes. He wanted to say something reassuring, anything at all that might ease the pain they were all feeling, but words failed him. The notion of walking through that door, of seeing the empty space where his mother should be, was almost too much to bear.

But he knew they had to go in. They had to face the reality of this first Christmas season without her, to honor her memory by continuing the traditions she had cherished. He turned to his family, trying to muster a smile, though his heart felt encumbered. "I know, sweetheart," he said, his voice thick with emotion. "I miss her too. But she would want us to be together, to celebrate as a family. We'll find a way to make this Christmas season special, for her and for us."

With that, they stepped out into the cold, their breath misting in the frosty air. Bob turned to his two sons and asked them if they could build a snowman for Grandpa since 'he must have been too busy this year.' They eagerly took on the challenge, leapt out of the car, and dug right in, rolling up large snowballs to create a lovely Christmas snowman for Grandpa. As Bob and his wife approached the front door, he hesitated for a moment, feeling the weight of the silence that greeted them. He opened the door, stepped inside, and immediately noticed the house lacking its familiar warmth. Some of the usual sights and smells were still there, but they were tinged with a bitterness, and they somehow felt hollow.

Bob's heart sank as he took in the sight of the unadorned Christmas tree standing alone in the corner of the living room. The boxes of decorations lay open on the floor, untouched and neglected. There was no fire crackling in the hearth, no comforting smell of cookies baking in the oven, and the air felt eerily still. It was like walking into a house caught in a moment of grief, a home that had lost its holiday spirit. The dim lighting cast long shadows, and the silence was weighty, broken only by the faint creaking of the floorboards under feet.

He glanced at Sherri, who met his eyes with a look of understanding and determination. They both knew they had to lift the spirits, not just for the sake of tradition but to bring some warmth and joy back into the home. Bob took a deep breath, putting on a brave face, and headed towards the kitchen where his father sat alone at the table. The older man looked up, his face a study in quiet grief, the lines of sorrow etched deeply into his features. He seemed smaller, more fragile than Bob remembered, the weight of loss evident in his slumped shoulders and the distant look in his eyes.

With a broad smile, Bob walked over and wrapped his arms around his father's shoulders, pulling him into a tight bear hug. "Hey, Pops! Merry Christmas, ya old man!" he said, infusing his voice with as much cheer as he could muster. His father startled slightly, then relaxed into the embrace, a faint smile touching his lips. "First ones here? How can we help?"

Bob's father turned to look at him, his eyes glistening with unshed tears. "It's... different without her," he murmured, his voice cracking.

Bob felt the lump in his throat grow, but forced a smile anyway, determined to bring some light back into the room. "Yeah, it is," he said softly. "But we're all here, and we can still make it special."

Meanwhile, Sherri moved with purpose, her presence a comforting and calming force. She found the stereo system and switched it on, filling the silence with the familiar strains of Christmas classics. The room seemed to brighten immediately, the music a melodic salve for their troubled hearts. She then knelt by the fireplace, expertly stacking the logs and striking a match. The flames roared to life, casting a warm glow that chased away the shadows. The room began to feel more alive, more like the Christmases they all remembered.

Sherri started pulling out the tangled strings of Christmas lights from the box, methodically unraveling them. She handed one end to Bob, and together they began to wind the lights around the tree. Their work was suddenly interrupted when the front door burst open with a flurry of excited voices. Bob's sons, along with their cousins, came charging in, their cheeks flushed with cold and their eyes sparkling with excitement.

"HEY, GRANDPA!" they shouted in unison, racing toward him. The children's exuberance was infectious, and their grandfather's face lit up with genuine joy for the first time that day. They surrounded him, hugged him tightly and all spoke at once describing the snowman they had just built for him outside.

"Come see it, come see it!" they insisted, tugging at his hands. Bob's father chuckled softly, allowing himself to be pulled to his feet. His eyes brightened at the sight of the children, his grandchildren, so full of life and energy. They led him towards the front door, their laughter resounding through the house.

As they reached the entryway, the door swung open, letting in a gust of cold air and the sound of more voices. Jason and George, with their wives, stepped inside, bringing with them a fresh burst of holiday cheer. They stomped the snow off their boots and were met with a cacophony of greetings and hugs. The hallway filled with the sound of laughter and happy chatter, as the house appeared to partially come alive once again.

Outside, the snow continued to fall softly, covering everything in a blanket of white. The children eagerly showed off their handiwork—a petite and jolly snowman, complete with a carrot nose, twigs for arms, and a row of small stones forming a slightly crooked smile. The adults admired the children's creation, the siblings seeing themselves in their young glowing faces. Bob's father watched the scene with a soft, wistful smile. He seemed to liven as he observed his family, his grief momentarily forgotten in the warmth of their togetherness.

Inside, Jason joined Bob in the kitchen. They opened the fridge with a sense of trepidation, half-expecting to find the usual abundance of holiday foods prepared by their mother. Instead, they were greeted with an alarming sight—empty shelves, a few sad-looking vegetables long past their prime, and a carton of milk that had soured. The pantry wasn't much better; what little food there was had expired, and there were telltale signs of neglect evident in the stale boxes and dusty cans. The brothers exchanged a worried glance, a silent acknowledgment of the severity of the situation.

Sherri continued her mission, now joined by the rest of the family. They embraced one another, holding on a little tighter than usual, the somber reality of the day settling over them. With quiet determination, they set to work decorating the tree, each ornament carefully chosen and placed with a reverence that spoke of their collective grief. As they hung the familiar baubles, they shared stories and memories, each ornament a conversation starter, a piece of their collective past. It wasn't long before the room was soon filled with the warm glow of lights and the tree was transformed into a dazzling centerpiece of holiday spirit. As the last ornament was hung and the tree topper placed, the family stepped back to admire their work. The tree stood proudly, a symbol of resilience and love, shining brightly against the backdrop of a difficult year.

As the evening progressed, Jason and George exchanged knowing glances with Bob and Sherri whenever they saw their father struggling with a simple task or when he tried to remember the details of a story he had told a hundred times before. It quickly became evident that things were not as they had hoped, and the reality of their father's condition was sinking in. George slipped outside, grabbing a snow shovel and set to work clearing the driveway and path to the front door. The snow was thick and heavy, but he worked methodically, pushing the packed white sheets aside.

Meanwhile, Jason and Bob continued their tour through the house, their concern growing with each discovery. The laundry basket was overflowing, with clothes left untouched for weeks and a sour smell. Bob hesitated before peeking into their father's bedroom, but when he did, the state of disarray broke his heart further. The bed was unmade, the sheets stained and musty. It was clear they hadn't been changed since their mother's passing. The room, once a place of comfort and rest, now felt cold and abandoned.

The decisive blow came when Bob opened the bathroom cabinet to check on his father's medication. The pill bottles were covered in a thin layer of dust, some still full, others barely touched. It was clear that his father hadn't been taking his medication as prescribed, a dangerous neglect that only heightened the alarm. The gravity of their father's deteriorating condition was undeniable. He had been putting up a brave front, insisting over the phone that he was fine, but the evidence told a different story. He was struggling, more than any of them had realized, and the façade he had maintained was crumbling before their eyes.

Jason and his wife decided to make a quick run to the grocery store. They grabbed their coats and keys, Jason giving Bob a reassuring squeeze on the shoulder before they left. They would stock up on food, not just for their Christmas dinner but enough to sustain their father in the coming weeks. As they drove off, Bob and Sherri set to work inside. Sherri headed to the laundry room, starting the first of many loads. The whir of the washing machine was a small comfort, a sound of things being put right, even if just a little.

As Bob continued to evaluate the condition of the disheveled house, he was overwhelmed with a mix of grief and guilt, and a tear slid down his cheek. His father had been lying, putting on a heroic face, not wanting to let on how tough it was to manage on his own. The truth was stark and painful. The thought of his father living in such neglect, laboring to cope with the loss of his wife and the responsibilities of daily life, was heart-wrenching. Bob knew they couldn't leave things as they were. His father needed help, more help than any of them could provide on their own.

The children played in the living room, their laughter and energy a welcome distraction from the gravity of the day. The adults shared quiet conversations, their eyes often drifting to the old man sitting quietly, trying to keep a smile, while his eyes reflected a deep sadness. As the day progressed, the siblings cleaned and organized, bringing a sense of familiarity back into the space, and soon the house began to feel warm again.

When the groceries arrived, the kitchen became a hub of commotion and excitement as everyone pitched in to prepare the holiday meal. The familiar aromas of roasted turkey, mashed potatoes, and fresh-baked bread began to fill the air, mingling with the scent of pine and the faint, sweet smell of cookies baking in the oven. The table was set with care, and the children helped place the plates and utensils, their excitement bubbling over.

As they sat down to eat, Bob looked around the table at his family, and his heart swelled with gratitude. They had come together, despite overwhelming sorrow and the empty space left by his mother's absence. Sure, it wasn't the same as it had been before, and it never would be again, but in that moment, surrounded by love and laughter, it just felt right. They were honoring her memory in the best way they knew how—by being together, supporting each other, and keeping her traditions alive.

The meal they shared was simple, but nourishing, and stories and laughter quickly filled the silent spaces around the table. They shared tears and smiles, and as the night wore on, the sadness softened, replaced by a quiet sense of peace. After dinner, they gathered around and each took a moment to place an extra ornament on the tree, a new tradition of remembrance. It was a small gesture, but it felt appropriate, a way to include her in the celebration she loved so much.

It was a different kind of Christmas celebration, one marked by the rawness of loss mixed with the fragile, sweet memories of a time that could never be again. It was so different from what it used to be, yet surrounded by his family, Bob felt a flicker of hope. They would carry on, not because it would be easy to do so, but because it was what she would have wanted. They would keep the traditions alive, not just for themselves, but for the love and joy she had given them all those years. And in that way, she would always be a part of their Christmas, a bright, enduring star in their family constellation.

As the fire crackled and the snow fell gently outside, Bob felt a sense of contentment settle over him. They had managed to turn the day around, to bring a little light into their father's darkened world. They had faced their grief and found a way to celebrate in spite of it. And as they sat there, basking in the warmth of the fire and the glow of the Christmas lights, he knew that they would be okay. It had been a tough day, but it was also a day of love and togetherness. Now the house felt more like a home, filled with love and memories, and as they got up and began to say their goodbyes, there was a quiet understanding among the siblings that things would need to change from here on out.

A week later, the brothers convened a "group meeting" over the phone. Each spoke from their respective homes dotted across the state. Bob sat at his kitchen table with a cup of coffee in hand. They discussed their father's condition, the state of the house, and the harsh reality that he could no longer manage alone. The conversation was difficult, filled with pauses and sighs, but they were united in their concern.

It quickly became clear that no one could quit their jobs to provide full-time care, and moving their father to another city to live with one of them just wasn't practical. The decision weighed heavily, but they knew what had to be done. They needed to find a place where their father could be cared for locally. It was a decision none of them had wanted to make, but his health and well-being was the priority.

With burdened hearts, but a renewed sense of resolve, they agreed to start looking for a suitable facility, a place where he could live comfortably and safely. The decision marked the beginning of a new chapter, one filled with uncertainty and change. They knew it would be an emotional journey, for them and their father, but it was necessary. The brothers promised to stay in close contact, to support each other and their father through this difficult transition.

As Bob hung up the phone, he looked around the house, now quiet and still. His family's decorations were still up, the tree twinkling softly in the corner. It had been a difficult Christmas, but the trip to Grandpa's house was a beautiful reminder of the strength of their family bond. They would face the challenges ahead together, just as they had done that day. For now, Bob resolved to visit more often, to ensure his father wasn't alone during this difficult time. They were embarking on a tough road, but they would navigate it together, holding onto the love and memories that had always sustained them.

The weeks following Christmas were a whirlwind of activity for the Harrison brothers. Each had taken on specific roles in the search for an appropriate assisted living facility for their father. They contacted placement agents, sifted through numerous brochures, and painstakingly compared costs and amenities. Every evening, they convened over video calls, discussing their findings, sharing thoughts on different facilities, and trying to gauge their father's emotional and physical state through their regular phone conversations with him. Despite their father's insistence that he was managing fine, the brothers couldn't ignore the numerous signs of decline they had witnessed during the holidays.

Then, on February 2, the situation escalated drastically. Bob was in the middle of a meeting at work when his phone rang. It was the police. His heart raced as the officer explained that their father had been in a car accident. The officer detailed that, thankfully, the accident had not resulted in any severe injuries to their father or others involved, but it was clear that their father could no longer safely drive. His license had been revoked on the spot, and he was being taken to the hospital to have a few minor wounds treated.

The news hit Bob like a tidal wave. He abruptly excused himself from the meeting, his mind racing. As he rushed to his car, he frantically called Sherri and his brothers, delivering the grim update. The conversations were a blur of concern and urgent coordination. Bob sped to the hospital, his mind swirling with worry and the stark realization that the time for a decision was no longer in the near future—it was now.

When Bob arrived at the hospital, he was greeted by a solemn-looking doctor who pulled him aside before he could see his father. The doctor explained that, given his father's current condition and the concerning state of his health they had observed, it was no longer safe for him to live alone. The car accident was a wake-up call; it highlighted the risks and underscored the need for full-time assisted care. The doctor handed Bob a list of recommended local facilities, noting that they had good reputations and specialized care that could cater to his father's needs.

Bob felt a surge of emotions envelop him—fear, sadness, and a sense of overwhelming responsibility. The decision he and his brothers had been inching toward was now unavoidable, and the weight of it pressed heavily on his chest. How could he possibly tell his broken father who had lost the love of his life that he would also be losing the home he had built decades of his most precious memories in, the place he felt most comfortable?

Bob took a deep breath, trying to compose himself before entering his father's hospital room. Inside, his father lay on the large bed, looking more fragile than ever. His face was pale, a few bruises marking his skin, and he seemed so much older and frailer than he had appeared just a little over a month ago. Bob pulled up a chair beside the bed, his heart aching at the sight. He gently took his father's hand, the touch grounding him in the moment. The room was quiet, save for the steady beeping of the heart monitor and the occasional rustle of nurses moving in the corridor outside.

A few hours passed before his father stirred, slowly opening his eyes. Bob smiled warmly, squeezing his father's hand. "Hey, Dad," he said softly. "How are you feeling?"

His father winced slightly, shifting in the bed. "A bit sore, but I'll be fine," he muttered, his voice weak but defiant. Bob could see the weariness in his eyes, a thin veneer of bravado masking the underlying fear and confusion.

They talked quietly, and Bob offered reassurances and comfort. He carefully broached the topic of the car accident, gently explaining the police's decision to revoke his father's license. His father sighed, a resigned look crossing his face. "I suppose it was bound to happen," he murmured, more to himself than to Bob. "Your mother always said I was getting too old for this."

Bob nodded, feeling that familiar lump form in his throat. He leaned in closer, his voice soft and steady. "We've been looking into some assisted living places, Dad. We want to make sure you're safe and taken care of. There's a really nice one nearby that we think you might like." His father looked at him, a mixture of sadness and acceptance in his eyes. He nodded slowly, not saying much, but his silence spoke volumes. The reality of his situation was settling in, and it was clear that, while he might not fully accept it yet, he vaguely understood.

In the following days, the brothers made the final arrangements. They settled on a nearby assisted living facility that came highly recommended. Bob and Sherri made a visit to check it out in person. The facility was impressive, almost overwhelming in its amenities and grandeur. As they entered, they were greeted by a massive chandelier hanging in the foyer, casting a bright, impressive light. The reception area buzzed with activity, an enormous contrast to the quiet desperation they had felt at their father's home.

They were given a tour of the big-box facility, guided by a friendly staff member who explained the various activities and services available to residents. As they surveyed the common areas, Bob imagined his father with other seniors engaged in a spirited game of pickleball on the court outside, or participating in a dance lesson in one of the activity rooms. There were swim classes, movie nights, and a calendar packed with social events. The tour concluded with a visit to what would be their father's new living space. The room was quaint and well-appointed, complete with a private bathroom and kitchenette. Some of the rooms they passed even had pets, cats and small dogs providing companionship for the residents.

Bob and Sherri exchanged relieved glances. It looked about as perfect as they could have hoped for—a place where their father could not only receive the care he needed but also find companionship and a sense of community. It felt like a place where he could not just survive but potentially thrive, making new friends and participating in activities that could bring him joy.

The decision, though difficult, was made with a sense of peace. They knew their father would be safe, supported, and perhaps even find happiness in this new chapter of his life. As they left the facility, Bob felt a bittersweet mix of relief and sorrow. They had found a solution, but it also marked the end of an era, a final acknowledgment that their father's independence was no longer feasible.

Returning to the hospital, Bob shared the news with his father, presenting the choice as an opportunity for a fresh start. His father listened quietly, reticently nodding along, the gravity of the situation settling in. There was a lingering sadness in his eyes, a yearning for the life he was leaving behind. The brothers and their families rallied around him, ensuring the transition would be as smooth and comforting as possible.

After signing the residency care plan, which outlined the details of their father's daily care and medical needs, the family prepared for the move. The next day, their father was transferred to the facility. The doctor had gone over his care plan, emphasizing the importance of new medications and physical therapy sessions that were to begin that week. Bob diligently took notes, feeling the weight of responsibility. He trusted the facility's staff to communicate effectively with their father's doctor, ensuring a smooth transition and continuity of care. The plan was meticulous, covering everything from medication schedules to therapy regimens, and Bob was determined to stay on top of it all.

The move to the assisted living facility was an emotional one, but started off as a positive experience. The staff seemed welcoming, the residents friendly, and slowly, their father appeared to adjust to his new surroundings. The brothers visited as often as their busy schedule would permit, bringing their children, sharing meals, and participating in some of the facility's events. It looked like a place where their father could find peace and companionship, and where the family could continue to create new memories together.

Over the coming weeks, as Bob walked through the facility, a few subtle details began to catch his attention, leaving him with a niggling sense of unease. Some of the caregivers, dressed in their uniforms, walked through the hallways with AirPods in their ears, seemingly disconnected from their surroundings. They didn't acknowledge the visitors or residents, their faces neutral, almost indifferent. The lack of smiles or greetings felt off-putting, a small but noticeable red flag. Moreover, every time they passed the indoor pool, it was eerily empty; meant to be a busy hub of activity, its waters were calm and lifeless. Despite the facility boasting an array of impressive amenities, it was curious that no one seemed to be using them.

These observations bothered Bob, a tiny seed of doubt planting itself in his mind. Yet he pushed them aside, reassuring himself that his father would find happiness here. Everything else had checked out; the facility was clean, the staff appeared competent, and the amenities, though underutilized, were top-notch. The cost, around $4,000 a month, was steep, but manageable when split among the brothers. They all agreed it was a worthy investment in their father's well-being. Given his proximity, Bob was designated as the primary point of contact, becoming the power of attorney and taking charge of the final decisions.

Bob made a personal commitment to visit his father every Friday after work. His brothers, living farther away, also pledged to visit more frequently. Despite the challenges of the past few months, the move brought a collective sigh of relief. The brothers felt they had made the right choice, providing their father with a supportive environment where he could find companionship and recover from the recent upheavals in his life. The thought of their father potentially thriving in this new setting brought them a sense of peace. They believed he might even become more active, taking advantage of the facility's amenities and programs. The burden of constant worry was temporarily lifted, replaced by cautious optimism.

They all hoped this new chapter would offer their father a chance to heal, both physically from his accident and emotionally from the loneliness that had followed their mother's passing. The facility seemed perfect on paper, and the brothers were excited about the possibilities, envisioning him making new friends, participating in activities, and regaining some of the joy and vitality that had faded in recent months. In the eyes of the brothers, the assisted living facility was a sparkling jewel, a place that seemed to offer everything their father could possibly need or want. It was beautifully maintained, with elegant common areas and a wide range of activities and amenities. Each time they visited, they couldn't help but express their admiration. "If I lived here, I'd be using the gym every single day," one of them would say, or, with a teasing grin, "Hey Dad, have you made any new girlfriends yet?" They laughed, winking at him, trying to lighten the mood and encourage him to embrace this new chapter.

But beneath this cautious optimism, Bob couldn't entirely shake the lingering doubts from his tours of the property. The unengaged staff, the unused amenities—these were small details, yet they clung to his thoughts like a shadow. As he drove away from the facility after settling his father in, a faint unease gnawed at him. He chose to ignore it, focusing instead on the positive aspects of the brothers' decision and the potential that lay ahead.

It wasn't long before that optimism was tested. The realities of life in the facility began to unfold in ways they hadn't anticipated, and the initial relief they felt gave way to a deeper, more troubling understanding of their father's new home. The journey they thought was nearing an end was, in fact, only beginning.

What Bob's brothers didn't realize was that their father wasn't using any of the amenities. He hadn't made any friends, and it was far from the spirited social environment they had imagined for him. Instead, he seemed completely overwhelmed by the vastness of the facility and the bustling activity that surrounded him. It was all too much, too fast, and he began retreating into the solitude of his room for days on end. He often forgot where he was; the unfamiliarity of his surroundings caused him to feel disoriented and lost. The staff, who seemed indifferent, didn't help. They referred to him impersonally as "Room 441," a number rather than a person, which only deepened his isolation and confusion.

Without anyone to connect with or guide him, he withdrew more and more. The dining hall, which was meant to be a place for socializing and enjoying meals, became a source of anxiety. The large, crowded space was intimidating, and he struggled with the noise and commotion. Instead of joining the other residents, he would slip into the small convenience store within the facility, purchasing snacks and prepackaged meals to eat alone in his room. His diet suffered as a result, and he wasn't drinking enough water or getting any exercise. The vibrant, active life the brothers had hoped for was slipping further out of reach.

Then came the shock of the first bill. Expecting the agreed-upon amount of $4,000, the brothers were stunned to see a total of $6,500. The bill read like this:

- Extra Food Delivery x 9 = $270
- Diapers/Changing x 65 = $130
- Dressing x 15 = $300
- Treatment for Wounds = $780
- Wellness Check x 6 = $450
- Medication Delivery x 30 = $570
- Base fee = $4,000
- TOTAL: $6,500

Yikes! This was far from what the brothers had anticipated. How had things gone so wrong? The shock of the inflated bill revealed some unsettling truths. Because their father wasn't attending meals in the dining hall and instead buying snacks from the small shop, he was being charged extra for every purchase. Additionally, since he wasn't collecting his medications at the scheduled times, there were additional fees for personalized delivery. The facility had neglected to explain these surcharges upfront, leaving the brothers blindsided. The unsettling thought that this might be a common practice for other residents gnawed at them.

They pored over the itemized charges. This wasn't what they had signed up for, and they were now faced with the unsettling realization that the facility wasn't as transparent or ideal as they had believed.

Had they made a mistake? Was their father truly being cared for, or was he just another number in a system that was more concerned with profit than with the well-being of its residents? The initial excitement and relief they had felt began to crumble, replaced by worry and doubt. They needed to get to the bottom of what was happening and ensure their father was not only safe but also happy and well-cared for. The brothers realized they needed to be more involved, to dig deeper into the facility's practices, and to find a way to truly support their father in this challenging transition.

Faced with the immediate demand to settle the bill, the brothers reluctantly paid the $6,500. They called the facility the next day, hoping to negotiate some flexibility in the pricing, to no avail. This financial strain was far more than they had bargained for, and it was already affecting their lives. Jason and Thomas, however, were notably absent when it came time to contribute. They didn't send their shares, leaving Bob and George to shoulder the burden alone.

The following day, Bob spoke with the facility's administration, hoping for some understanding or compromise. The response he received was chilling. They explained that the facility wasn't equipped to accommodate each resident's individual needs outside of the standard schedule. If their father couldn't adhere to the routine, the extra costs were unavoidable. Bob was stunned. They were paying a premium price for what was supposed to be top-tier care, yet the facility seemed to lack the staff and resources to offer any real flexibility. The reality was stark: either their father conformed to the set schedule, or they would continue to face exorbitant charges each month. Bob felt a surge of frustration and helplessness. How could this be happening at such an expensive and supposedly reputable place?

As the months passed, the financial strain deepened. Bob had to make significant sacrifices to cover the unexpected expenses. He cut back on his quarterly golf outings, much to the disappointment of his friends, who missed their regular get-togethers. It had been his outlet, a chance to unwind and decompress, but now it was gone. Sherri, his wife, had been promised a new car for her birthday—a promise Bob had been making for two years. That dream was now indefinitely postponed. Their children, accustomed to the annual family vacation to Palm Beach, were devastated when Bob informed them that the trip was off, not just for this year but likely for the foreseeable future. The kids were furious, feeling the loss of something they looked forward to all year. They let him know their frustration in no uncertain terms, their anger and disappointment adding to Bob's already heavy burden.

The brothers were now grappling with the harsh realities of caring for their aging father. They had believed they were providing him with the best possible care. Instead, they found themselves entangled in a system that seemed more concerned with profit than with genuine care. The emotional and financial toll was immense, and the once-hopeful optimism they felt had been replaced by a grim determination to navigate this unexpected challenge. They knew they had to reassess their approach, but the question loomed: what could they do differently? The weight of their father's well-being—and the impact on their own lives—pressed down on Bob with increasing intensity.

He understood that sacrifices were necessary to ensure his father's comfort, but the strain was palpable. What troubled him most was the lack of involvement from his siblings. He felt like he was carrying the burden alone. All the promises his brothers had made—to visit more often, to share the costs, to be more present—had fallen short. Some months, Bob was the only visitor, and he often ended up covering the bills himself. His brothers offered excuses, citing work, family, or distance, and it hurt. Bob knew it must hurt their father too, though he rarely said anything about it. Despite this, Bob never missed his weekly Friday visits, cherishing the time spent with his dad.

One Friday, as Bob walked into the facility, he passed the eerily quiet pool. It was always empty, devoid of the laughter and splashing he had envisioned when they first chose the place. When he reached his father's room, he asked, "Dad, how are you enjoying it here? Do you get to play pickleball? Go to dance lessons? How about swimming or any of the other activities?"

His father's response was slow and tired. "Oh, son, it's too much. It's hard for me to get up and out of bed." The reality hit

Bob harder than he expected. The accident had taken a greater toll on his father than any of them had realized. The man who had once been vibrant and social now struggled with even the simplest of activities. The mention of pickleball or dance lessons seemed almost laughable in this context. It became clear that his father was not engaging with the facility's amenities at all.

Bob had always known his father to be a sociable person, someone who loved connecting with others. It was painful to see him withdrawn, not just because of the physical limitations from the accident but because he wasn't participating in activities. The change in his father had begun after his mother passed away, but the accident had accelerated the decline. Bob had hoped that the community atmosphere of the facility would encourage his father to be more active and social, but it seemed the opposite was happening.

The reality of his situation was profound; his father was not just physically diminished, but he was emotionally and socially retreating as well. The place that was supposed to be a haven for him, offering companionship and activity, had instead become a gilded cage, trapping him in a cycle of isolation and inactivity. Bob felt a mix of sadness and frustration, wondering if there was more he could do to help his father regain some joy and purpose. He couldn't shake the feeling that something fundamental had been lost, something that no amount of luxurious amenities could replace.

Bob tried to encourage his father to participate in the facility's activities, hoping it would rekindle some of his old spark. He pulled up the activities calendar and read off the upcoming events, his voice enthusiastic and hopeful. When his father's eyes finally lit up at the mention of an arts and crafts event on Tuesday, they both felt a hint of optimism. Bob left that day with a lighter heart, hopeful that this small step might help his father engage with the world around him.

However, when Bob returned the following week and asked how the arts and crafts event had gone, his father's response was a crushing disappointment. "No one came to get me," his father explained, his voice tinged with resignation. The anger rose in Bob, a hot, bubbling frustration that tightened his chest. It was becoming increasingly clear that his father was not just physically limited but was also being neglected in a place paid to care for him. His reclusiveness was deepening, and the robust man Bob once knew was fading away, losing the flame that had defined him for so long.

Bob couldn't contain his frustration. Just twenty minutes later, he spotted a caregiver walking down the hallway. She had AirPods in, oblivious to his shouts. He chased her down, tapping her on the shoulder to get her attention. Startled, the caregiver removed an earbud and looked at him expectantly. Bob quickly explained the situation, how his father had wanted to attend the arts and crafts session but hadn't been taken there.

The caregiver's response was disheartening. "What's his room number?" she asked, almost mechanically.

"Room 441," Bob replied, trying to keep his voice steady.

The caregiver sighed. "Well, you see, Room 441 doesn't like to leave his room, and he needs assistance when it's time to go anywhere. We don't have the staff to take each person to the events they want to attend. They have to get up and come to the activities room on their own, and since he can't, that's going to be tough. But I wasn't on shift on Tuesday, so I'll leave a note for whoever is in next week! Good to see ya!" With that, she turned away, putting her AirPod back in and continuing down the hall.

Bob stood there, stunned. His jaw dropped in disbelief. This was supposed to be a premier facility, the best money could buy, yet his father was being treated like a number, a task to be managed rather than a person to be cared for. His father was being left to rot in his room, devoid of social interaction, mental stimulation, or even basic care. The caregivers didn't even bother to learn his name, referring to him simply by his room number. The realization was heartbreaking and infuriating.

As Bob walked back to his father's room, a deep sadness settled over him. His heart ached as he wondered if this was the grim reality of end-of-life care. Was this really all there was? The bright hopes he once had for this facility, for a place where his father could thrive and find joy again, were now ashes. This place, once seen as a haven, felt more like a sterile, impersonal hell. Bob's optimism crumbled, replaced by a grim understanding of the neglect and isolation his father was experiencing. The weight of the situation was crushing, and he felt a desperate need to find a better way, though what that could be, he didn't yet know.

The next Friday, Bob came to see his father. Feeling resigned for the moment to this new mournful paradigm, yet wanting to project positivity, he gently asked, "Dad, how have you been? Have you made any new friends this week? Maybe met a nice lady or a gentleman to chat with?"

His father looked up, eyes clouded with sadness and resignation, and slowly shook his head. "Bob," he began, his voice thick with emotion, "all my friends... they're gone. They've all passed away. I don't want to get close to anyone else, only to lose them again." The words hit Bob like a punch to the gut, leaving him breathless. It was an aching realization that pierced his heart, filling him with a deep, relentless sorrow. This wasn't just about the lack of comfort or the subpar care; it was about the profound loneliness and despair his father felt, surrounded by reminders of loss and fleeting connections.

As Bob listened, a wave of guilt washed over him, heavier than he'd ever felt. How had he let it come to this? The thought of leaving him there, day after day, tore at Bob's soul. The care felt cold, the staff distant and disinterested, and the atmosphere suffocating. It was clear to him that this facility, despite its glossy brochures and exorbitant price, was failing his father in the most fundamental ways. As he left that evening, he made a silent vow, a promise that burned with determination: he would find something better. His father deserved more than just a place to stay; he deserved a place to feel joy, to be seen, and to thrive.

That night, as Bob walked through the door of his own home, Sherri, his wife, immediately sensed something was wrong. She saw the pain etched on his face and the burden of his emotions. Without a word, Bob collapsed into her arms, the dam breaking as tears flowed freely. He poured out his heart, describing the bleak reality of his father's situation—the indifference of the caregivers, the loneliness, and the over-inflated costs that seemed to pay for nothing but heartache. "Sherri," he painfully muttered, "I can't leave him there. It's like a prison—it's not a home. I wouldn't wish that place on my worst enemy, let alone my own father. I'd rather die than end up in a place like that." Sherri held him tighter, her heart breaking for both Bob and his father. They sat together, sharing a tender moment, their love and concern intertwining in quiet resolve. Bob knew they had to act. This wasn't just a matter of finding a different facility; it was about giving his father back his dignity, his joy, his life.

The next day, fueled by a renewed sense of purpose, Bob reached out to his brothers. Despite the recent distance and lack of involvement, he knew they needed to come together for their father's sake. He called each of them, his voice steady but urgent. "We need to find something better for Dad," he told them. "He's not doing well, and we can't leave him in that place. It's not just about the money; it's about the quality of life. He deserves better."

Thomas, the practical one, immediately agreed to dive into research, promising to set up a group chat where they could all share information. George, always quick with suggestions, sent over a list of four other facilities nearby. Jason, the youngest, mentioned something he had heard about—Residential Assisted Living, a concept that seemed more personal and compassionate, and he promised to look into it further. As the brothers began to collaborate, Bob felt a sliver of hope. They were finally uniting around a common goal, driven by their shared love for their father.

The following Friday had been relentless, the kind of day where every task stretched into an ordeal. Bob glanced at the clock, his stomach sinking as he realized how late it had gotten. He was supposed to visit his dad at the facility, a routine he never missed. Rushing, he dialed the facility's number, hoping to let them know he was on his way. No answer. He tried again, but the phone just rang. Bob reassured himself, thinking, *It'll be fine; they should still let me in.*

When he finally arrived, breathless and anxious, he was met with the cold reality at the front desk. The staff member, disinterested and firm, informed him that visiting hours were over. "I'm sorry, sir, but you can't see him now."

Bob's face flushed with frustration. "Are you kidding me? I called! I just want to see my dad," he pleaded. The receptionist didn't budge, repeating the policy as if reading from a script. Bob's anger boiled over. He slammed his fists on the counter, the sound echoing through the empty reception area. "This is ridiculous!" he shouted, feeling weeks of frustration bubbling up inside him.

Desperate and defeated, Bob stepped outside to call his dad, his hands shaking. When his father answered, Bob apologized, explaining he couldn't visit that night but would come tomorrow. He tried to keep his voice steady, but his dad's response—a quiet, "I understand, son"—carried a sadness that pierced Bob's heart. He could hear the loneliness, the disappointment in his father's tone, and it crushed him. Bob hung up, barely holding back tears. He had forgotten that tomorrow was his daughter's ballet recital, but a promise was a promise. He would be there for his dad, no matter what.

The next morning, Bob arrived at the facility bright and early. He checked in, the front desk staff now a different, less cold face, and made his way to room 441. Bob had never visited on a Saturday, always preferring the quieter weekdays, but today was special. He was determined to make up for the missed visit. As he entered his father's room, he was greeted with a warm smile. The sight of his dad, frail but still so full of spirit, filled Bob with a bittersweet joy.

Determined to make the day memorable, Bob helped his father into a wheelchair, and they headed downstairs. They spent hours in the activities room, playing chess, just as they had so many times before. Bob felt a wave of nostalgia, remembering all the times his dad had patiently taught him. It was his father who taught him everything, how to shoot hoops, hit a baseball, and score a goal. The memories washed over him, a mix of happiness and sorrow. His father would doze off between chess moves, his energy waning, but Bob cherished every moment, every quiet breath, every sleepy smile.

For lunch, they ventured to the food hall. They sat together, sharing a meal, watching an instructor lead a nearly empty Zumba class nearby. Bob smiled as they observed three elderly women trying to follow along, classical music echoing through the barren room. It was a rare moment of peace in his life filled with deadlines and obligations. Bob felt grateful to be there, to share this with his dad. They didn't need words; the shared silence was enough, filled with an unspoken understanding and love.

As they returned to the fourth floor, Bob noticed tears in his father's eyes. Concerned, he knelt beside the wheelchair and gently asked, "Dad, what's wrong?"

His father, voice heavy with emotion, said, "This has been the best day I've had since I came here." The words hit Bob like a sledgehammer. Two years. Two years in this place, and this was the best day? A day filled with simple joys, nothing extraordinary, yet it stood out in contrast to the monotony and isolation of his father's daily life.

The realization was gut-wrenching. Bob hugged his dad tightly, promising himself that this couldn't be the way his father lived out his days. He knew now, more than ever, that they needed to find a better place, somewhere his dad could truly enjoy life. The staff here were too few, too rushed, and too uncaring to provide the assistance and companionship his father needed. His dad deserved to be more than just another resident; he deserved to be seen, to be cared for, to be loved.

Driving home, Bob couldn't hold back his tears. It had been a beautiful day, filled with laughter and love, yet it ended on such a sour note. The thought of leaving his dad in that place felt unbearable. Bob prayed that his brothers would be able to find something better. The drive home was long, and Bob cried the entire way, heartache filling his chest.

The following week, Jason was in town, and he and Bob decided to visit their dad together on Saturday. They entered the familiar, sterile environment of the facility, hoping to brighten their father's day. However, it quickly became apparent that their dad wasn't feeling well. He seemed listless, his countenance dulled by a vague discomfort. So, they stayed in his room, chatting quietly and trying to lift his spirits.

After a few hours, Jason glanced around, a puzzled expression crossing his face. He turned to Bob, his voice low but insistent. "Is it just me, or has there been no action on this floor?"

Bob looked at him, confused. "What do you mean?"

Jason leaned closer, lowering his voice even more. "I mean, not one caregiver has come by to check on us. No one's asked if Dad needs anything, or if we're okay. Isn't that kind of... crazy?" He paused before adding, with a hint of disbelief, "Aren't you paying an arm and a leg for this place?"

The question hit Bob hard; frustration welled up inside him. It was a sore point, as he was, in fact, paying an arm and a leg. Supposedly, all the brothers were splitting the cost, but Bob knew he was shouldering more than his fair share. He had sacrificed so much for this arrangement. His weekends spent on the golf course, his family vacations, even the little luxuries that brought joy to his wife and kids—all gone. Bob had tightened the family budget, altered their lifestyle, and made countless sacrifices to afford his father's care. Bob looked around, trying to see the situation through Jason's fresh eyes. He hadn't noticed the lack of attention anymore; he'd become numb to it. It was a painful acknowledgment, but Jason was right. The absence of staff presence was glaring. Bob's mind raced with the thought of what it would be like to bring Dad home, to give him the love and attention he deserved. But deep down, he knew it wasn't feasible. The level of care his father needed was beyond what he could provide on his own, especially with the demands of work and family life.

Breaking the heavy silence, Jason pulled out his phone and started talking about something he had been researching, Residential Assisted Living. He explained that he had found some promising alternatives, including one just around the corner from this facility. The cost was similar, but the key difference was the caregiver-to-resident ratio—only four to one, which was much better than the current situation. He hadn't scheduled a tour yet, but he described the smaller home setting as potentially a better fit for their dad. It wasn't fancy; there were no grand chandeliers or luxurious amenities, but it seemed warm and welcoming. The owners' faces were right on the website, and they had a personal story—having opened the home because their own father needed care. This detail struck a chord with Bob. It sounded genuine, a place built out of love and necessity.

The brothers agreed to visit the RAL home the following week. As they pulled up to the modest, welcoming house, Bob felt a renewed sense of hope. Inside, they were greeted by a cozy atmosphere. Their dad would have his own bedroom and bathroom, and while there wasn't a kitchenette, meals were served family-style, fostering a sense of community among the eight residents. Two caregivers were always on shift, ensuring personalized attention, with a manager overseeing the operations. The owner was there to give them the tour, and they instantly connected, bonding over their shared experiences and love for their fathers.

Despite the absence of grand facilities, the home was lively. The activities calendar was full, offering plenty of engaging options for the residents. It was a stark contrast to the impersonal, institutional feel of their current setup. This felt like a real home, a place where their father could find companionship, care, and comfort. As they talked with the owner, their initial optimism grew into genuine excitement. This was it—this was the place their father deserved to be.

Finishing the tour, Bob and Jason felt a profound sense of peace for the first time in a long while. They were thrilled with this option, certain that it would bring their father the happiness and care he needed. They called their other brothers on the drive home, voices filled with relief and excitement as they shared the news. Jason had to fly out the next day, but they all agreed: Bob would handle the transition to the Residential Assisted Living home. The brothers felt united in their decision, hopeful for a brighter future for their dad. The burdens of the past months seemed lighter, replaced by a renewed sense of hope and determination.

Bob was bursting with excitement the next day, eager to tell his dad the good news. They had finally found a place where he wouldn't be reduced to a number but treated with dignity and respect. However, when he tried to call, there was no answer. He dialed again, and again, but for six long hours, he heard nothing but the unanswered ringing. Anxiety gnawed at him. This wasn't like his dad, who usually kept his phone close. Bob's worry escalated into panic. He called the facility's front desk, his heart pounding as he awaited their response.

The woman who answered the phone spoke in a monotone, delivering the news that Bob's father had been moved to a hospital. Bob's blood ran cold. "Moved? Why?" he demanded, his voice trembling. The woman hesitated before revealing that his father had fallen the night before. It had taken 14 hours for anyone to find him. He had lain there, alone and in pain, on the cold, hard floor. The fall had resulted in a broken arm, a fractured rib, and, worst of all, bleeding in his brain. The shock and horror of the situation hit Bob like a tidal wave.

He was furious. "WHAT THE HELL!?" he yelled into the phone, the anger and fear boiling over. "How did this happen? Why wasn't I notified? How could no one have found him for 14 hours? And where is he now?" The receptionist, seemingly indifferent, explained that his father had been transferred to the hospital down the road two hours earlier and that was all the information she could provide. Bob slammed the phone down, grabbed his wife Sherri and the kids, and rushed to the hospital, his mind racing with worry and rage.

At the hospital, the family was met by a doctor who took them aside. The doctor's face was grim as he explained the situation. If someone had found Bob's father sooner, they might have been able to relieve the pressure caused by the brain bleed. But it was too late. His father was alive, but barely. The damage was severe, and there was little hope for recovery. The doctor's words blurred in Bob's mind, his world shattering around him. His father was now in a vegetative state. The prognosis was bleak; there was nothing they could do to bring him back.

Bob's children, silent and tearful, went in to sit beside their beloved grandfather. Sherri stood at the door, her eyes welling with tears as she looked at the frail figure lying in the hospital bed. She tried to keep it together, but the sight was too much, and she began to cry softly. Bob stood there, paralyzed with a torrent of emotions—anger, guilt, frustration, and a deep, gnawing resentment. For two years, he had devoted his time, energy, and resources to ensuring his father's well-being. He had sacrificed so much, and just when they had found a place that felt right, it was too late. His father was slipping away, ready to join his mother on the other side. The weight of it all was just too much to handle.

Sherri joined the children by his father's bedside, offering what comfort she was able. Bob, struggling to keep his emotions in check, pulled out his phone to text his brothers. He explained the situation as best he could, urging them to drive in as soon as possible to say their final goodbyes. He felt a numbness settle over him as he hit send, a heavy sense of finality pressing down on him.

As he prepared to enter the room, a doctor approached him. "Mr. Hayes," the doctor began cautiously, "may I ask where your father was staying?" Bob mentioned the name of the facility, and immediately, the doctor's expression darkened. "Geez," the doctor muttered, shaking his head. "I wish I could have told you about some local Residential Assisted Living homes. They're so much better for situations like your dad's. They offer more personalized care, and the attention to each resident is so much higher. These big facilities... they're just not equipped for this kind of care. They take your money and leave you feeling helpless. I'm terribly sorry."

The doctor's words stung, confirming Bob's worst fears. The neglect, the lack of communication, the inadequate care—all of it had led to this heartbreaking situation. Bob felt a surge of regret, a desperate wish that they could have found a better place sooner. Now, as he stood on the brink of losing his father, he was consumed with sorrow and rage, a deep sense of injustice that this was how his father's story was ending.

The next day, the waiting room was stifling with unspoken words and unexpressed emotions. Bob felt like a pressure cooker about to explode. As his brothers arrived one by one, families in tow, to say their goodbyes, he could barely muster the energy to speak to them. Each sibling's arrival brought a fresh wave of resentment crashing over him. Where had they been when Dad needed them most? Where were they when *he* needed them? The anger bubbled up, raw and visceral, as he watched them mourn a father they had largely abandoned to his care.

Bob hadn't realized the extent of his fury until he saw his father lying there frail and broken, surrounded by family desperate to speak with him once more. His rage wasn't just about the lack of help; it was also about the missed opportunities, the years of shared responsibility that never materialized. The resentment pulsed inside him with each sympathetic hug and murmured condolence. It was suffocating. "What if," he thought bitterly, "…what if we had all been there for Dad? What if we had been vigilant together, seen the signs, and moved him to a better place sooner?" The questions gnawed at him, each "what if" like a dagger twisting in his gut. He couldn't shake the image of his father alone on that cold floor, suffering in silence. The anger wasn't just at his siblings—it was at himself, for not being able to save his father from this fate.

For two agonizing days, Bob simmered in this cauldron of emotion as his brothers and their families came and went, sharing memories and shedding tears. He could hardly look at them. It was a continuous reminder of their collective failure. His mind was a whirlwind of guilt and frustration. He felt like he was drowning in a sea of regrets, and each brother was an anchor dragging him further down.

Then, the inevitable happened. In the quiet hours of the next morning, their father passed away. The room was filled with a strange, hollow silence. Bob felt an unexpected sense of relief wash over him. A small buoy of relief amidst a sea of sorrow, but it was there nonetheless. The long, burdensome vigil was over, and with it, the weight of responsibility lifted slightly from his shoulders. It was a bittersweet end to a difficult journey.

Bob felt an overwhelming mix of gratitude and sorrow as he reflected on the last two years he spent with his father. These years had been more precious and intimate than the thirty before them. In those fleeting moments, Bob cherished the chance to reconnect, to reminisce, and to simply be present. But intertwined with these treasured memories was a gnawing sense of regret and guilt. It was a burden he carried quietly, a shadow that darkened his joy.

From the very first visit to the facility where his father resided, Bob sensed that something was amiss. The care, though adequate on the surface, was lacking in warmth and thoroughness. Yet he pushed those feelings aside, convincing himself that it was enough, that his father would be okay. As the bills came in, revealing hidden charges for every small service, Bob's unease grew. Still, he didn't challenge the system, didn't demand better, didn't advocate fiercely enough for his father's needs. The weekends, which were supposed to be filled with connection and comfort, often felt hollow, marked by brief and distant interactions with the few caregivers on the clock.

Bob's heart ached with the weight of this perceived failure. Unlike the grief he felt when his mother passed away—a sadness tempered by the knowledge that she had been well-cared for—this grief was laced with self-recrimination. He couldn't shake the feeling that he had let his father down, that he hadn't done enough. The guilt was suffocating, a constant reminder of the moments he missed, the actions he didn't take, the voices he silenced—his own and his father's.

In the stillness of his reflection, Bob understood a profound truth. The allure of large assisted living facilities often lies in their impressive facades: the elegant décor, the expansive list of amenities, the promise of a dynamic social life. But behind these glittering surfaces, the reality can be starkly different. The resident-to-caregiver ratio is often skewed, leaving many elderly residents without the attentive care they truly need. For those who are less mobile or less social, the grand amenities become meaningless, a mere showpiece for visiting family members rather than a practical benefit for the residents themselves.

Bob learned, through painful experience, that these facilities often entice families with a seemingly reasonable entry rate, only to burden them with additional charges for essential services. It's a strategy that preys on the emotions of families desperate for a solution, who may not see the true cost until it's too late. The focus on profit over care became glaringly apparent, leaving Bob feeling betrayed by an industry that promised so much but delivered so little.

In the end, the true lesson Bob took away was one of vigilance and advocacy. The aesthetics of a facility, the polished sales pitches, the glossy brochures—these are not the measures of quality care. It's the human touch, the genuine compassion, the ratio of caregivers to residents that matter most. Visiting at different times, speaking with medical professionals who interact with these facilities, reading reviews from other families—these steps are crucial in truly understanding the quality of care being provided.

KEY TAKEAWAYS

Bob's story serves as a cautionary tale for others in similar situations. Trust your instincts. If something feels wrong from the beginning, don't ignore those feelings. There are alternatives, often smaller, more personalized care homes that prioritize the well-being of their residents over profit margins. It's essential to do thorough research, ask the hard questions, and never settle for less than what your loved one deserves. Bob wishes he had listened to his gut, spoken up more forcefully, and taken action when he had the chance. It's a heavy burden to carry, but sharing his story might help others avoid the same mistakes, ensuring that their loved ones receive the care and dignity they deserve in their final years.

CHAPTER 5:
TURNING POINT

*"How empathy and innovation transform
the approach to care"*

Susan had always been a pillar of faith and community, a woman whose dedication to her church and her family was unwavering. She was a familiar face every Sunday, never missing a service, as she cherished the peace and spiritual connection she found in the Lord's presence especially through her divorce. Raised in a devout Christian family, Susan learned early on the importance of faith, prayer, and fellowship. Her parents, Linda and Dennis, instilled in her a deep reverence for their beliefs, and Sundays were a sacred time for them. They would sit together in the wooden pews, their voices rising in song and prayer, a family united in devotion.

As Susan grew up and started her own family, she was determined to impart these same values to her children. She enrolled them in a Christian private school, where they could learn and grow in an environment steeped in faith. Summers were marked by the excitement of church camps, where they could immerse themselves in spiritual activities and forge lifelong friendships. Every weekend, Susan faithfully brought her children to Sunday school, where they learned Bible stories and sang hymns. She wanted them to experience the same love and comfort that she had always found in her faith community. Beyond her role as a mother, Susan was an active member of her church. She led a women's Bible study every Tuesday night, a time she cherished dearly. It was more than just a study group; it was a circle of friends, a support system, a place where they could delve into God's word and share their lives with one another. The room would often be filled with laughter, tears, and heartfelt discussions as they navigated life's challenges together. Susan found immense joy in these gatherings, relishing the camaraderie and the deep sense of purpose she felt in guiding these women through their spiritual journeys.

One particular Tuesday, the group was gathered in Susan's cozy living room, a space filled with the warmth of flickering candles and the sweet smell of brownies just out of the oven. As they shared prayer requests, Amy, one of the women in the group, spoke up, her voice strained with worry. She revealed that her mother's dementia was worsening and that she feared the time was soon approaching when she would need to move to an assisted living facility for round-the-clock support. The group collectively exhaled a sigh of empathy, their hearts aching for Amy. Many of them understood all too well the pain and confusion that came with watching a loved one slowly slip away. The women offered words of comfort, prayer, and aid, expressing their willingness to be there for Amy in any way she needed.

During the conversation, another member mentioned a new Residential Assisted Living home that was being built nearby. She spoke highly of the place, noting its comfy environment and dedicated staff. She encouraged Amy to visit the facility and even offered to accompany her, understanding the daunting nature of such decisions. The discussion about aging parents and the care they required struck a chord with many in the group, including Susan. Although her parents were still relatively healthy, she couldn't help but think of them and the inevitability of time. As the evening wound down, the women began gathering their things, hugging one another goodbye.

Just then, Susan's phone rang. It was her father, Dennis. His voice was shaky and breathless, immediately putting Susan on edge. There was a tremor in his words that she had never heard before. "Your mother isn't waking up... Susan, help, please help." His words were fractured with raw emotion. The gravity of the moment hit Susan like a tidal wave. The unthinkable thought that her mother, Linda, the woman who had been her rock, her guide, her best friend, might be... gone. Susan's face went pale, her legs were like noodles, and she felt as if the ground had disappeared beneath her feet. Immediately, the women noticed the sudden change in her demeanor and gathered around, their visages full of concern.

Struggling to find her voice, she managed to say, "D-d-dad, I'll be right there." She hung up the phone with trembling hands and hurriedly began to gather her things. The women around her, sensing the urgency and distress, implored to know what had happened and how they could help.

Tears welled up in Susan's eyes as she whispered, "I think my mom… just… passed away. I need to go see them, and I… I don't know." Her voice broke, and she collapsed to her knees, her sobs wracking her body. The realization hit her with full force, shattering her composure. Could it be real…her mother, the woman who had always been there, who had taught her everything, could she really be gone?

The women around her moved closer, laying hands on her, their voices lifting in prayer. They prayed for peace, for strength, for Susan's heart to be comforted by the knowledge that her mother was now in heaven, free from pain and embraced by angels. They prayed for Dennis, for the family, for the wisdom to navigate the difficult days ahead. Susan felt their hands, their prayers, and the presence of God wrapping around her like a warm blanket. It was a moment of deep, personal and spiritual connection, a lifeline thrown to her as she gathered her bearings in a swirling sea of despair. After what felt like an eternity, the prayers began to quiet, and Susan, her limbs still trembling, found a small measure of calm. She thanked her friends through her tears, grateful for their support. They helped her to her feet, and made sure she was steady enough to leave. As she walked to her car, her heart ached with an overwhelming fear of what awaited her, so thankful for the women who surrounded her with a deep sense of love and community, a reminder that she was not alone.

As she drove, her mind raced with anxiety as a flood of memories washed over her. She prayed silently, asking God for strength and clarity, for her father, for her family. The house loomed in the distance, and as she pulled into the driveway, she took a deep breath. Whatever awaited her inside, she knew she would face it with the same faith and courage that had always guided her… that her sweet courageous mother had instilled in her.

Susan entered her parents' home. The sound of her father's heart-wrenching cries echoed down the hallway, a painful wail that tore through the quiet stillness of the night. The sorrowful noise grew louder as she approached the bedroom, her hands felt limp and clammy, and she felt her stomach tighten with dread. She paused for a moment outside the door, gathering her strength. Taking a deep breath, she gently pushed the door open, revealing a scene that shattered her heart. Inside, her father Dennis was kneeling by the bed, his body convulsing with inconsolable sobbing. He clung to the lifeless form of his beloved wife, Linda, who lay still and peaceful on the bed. Her eyes were closed, her expression serene, as if she had simply drifted into a gentle sleep. But the pallor of her skin and the coldness of her touch told a different story. Linda was gone. The woman who had been Susan's anchor, her cherished mother, was no longer alive. Susan felt heavy waves of grief wash over her. This was the moment she had dreaded but never truly prepared for.

She quietly walked into the room, her footsteps muffled on the carpet. Kneeling beside her father, she gently placed a hand on his shoulder, offering what comfort she could. He looked up at her, his eyes red and swollen with tears, his face marked with the pain of a man who had lost the love of his life. Without a word, Susan leaned down and kissed her mother's cool cheek. The reality of the situation settled in her chest like a stone.

"How did this happen?" she asked softly, her voice barely above a whisper. Dennis, still shaking with grief, struggled to find his words. He recounted the events of the evening with a tremor in his voice, his gaze fixed on Linda's peaceful face. After dinner,

Linda had mentioned a headache and asked to lie down. He had helped her into bed, tucking her in as he always did, and then went back to the kitchen to clean up. Afterward, he had settled into his chair to watch a TV show, but soon drifted off to sleep. When he awoke, the house was quiet, and the clock showed it was nearly 8 p.m. Concerned by the silence, he had gone to check on Linda.

"As soon as I walked in," Dennis stammered, his voice breaking, "I knew something was wrong. She looked so pale... and cold." He paused, struggling with the memory. "I shook her, called her name, tried everything... but she didn't respond. She was gone." He collapsed into Susan's arms, his unrestrained sobs caused his body to tremble.

Susan held him tightly, her own tears streaming down her face. The weight of the loss settled heavily between them. Dennis and Linda had been together since high school, a love story that had spanned decades. They had faced life's joys and sorrows together, always side by side. Their love had been a constant in Susan's life, a beacon of stability and warmth. As they grew older, their love had only deepened, transforming into a tender, caring partnership. They had become inseparable, looking after one another in the most endearing ways—holding doors open, helping each other with daily tasks, cooking meals together, and reminding each other to take their medication. Their bond was a beautiful, enduring testament to true love and devotion.

With a deep breath, Susan gently broke the embrace and looked into her father's eyes. "Dad," she said softly, "we need to call someone to take care of Mom's body." She spoke with a calm firmness, trying to be the steady presence her father needed. "But I'll stay here with you. We'll get through this together."

Dennis nodded, too overcome with grief to speak anymore. Susan pulled out her phone and called the necessary services, her voice steady even as her heart ached. She then called her ex-husband, explaining the situation in a few concise words. She asked him to either pick up their children from her house or stay with them, as she didn't want them to be alone when they learned about their grandmother's passing. Her ex-husband agreed without hesitation, offering his condolences and support. Susan thanked him, grateful for his understanding and help.

Within an hour, a discreet van arrived to take Linda's body. The scene was quiet and respectful, with the professionals handling everything with the utmost care. Susan stood by her father, holding his hand, as they watched the last earthly remains of her mother leave their home. The finality of it all hit Susan hard, but she stayed composed, knowing her father needed her strength.

Afterward, she led Dennis to the living room, where they sat together in silence, the weight of the moment hanging heavily in the air. Susan sent a brief message to the women in her Bible study group, informing them of her mother's passing and thanking them for their prayers and support. She knew she could rely on their comfort and encouragement in the coming weeks.

As she sat there with her father, Susan reflected on the love her parents had shared, the life they had built together, and the deep impact her mother's loss would have on all who knew her. She was acutely aware of the void her mother's passing would leave in their lives. Her parents' love had been something to aspire to, a gentle reminder of what it meant to truly care for another person. The thought of her father navigating life without his lifelong partner was almost unbearable. It was going to be a difficult road ahead, but she knew they would face it together, supported by their faith, family, and friends. For now, all they could do was hold on to each other and cherish the memories of a beautiful life well-lived.

The next morning, Susan woke up early, determined to be the pillar of strength her father needed, wanting to show him how much he was loved. Though her heart was in agony and her movements were labored, she quietly moved around the kitchen, preparing breakfast with as much care as she could muster. The smell of sizzling bacon soon filled the house, and she squeezed fresh oranges into a pitcher, wanting to bring a little bit of sunshine into this gloomy morning. As she whisked eggs and set out fresh fruit, her mind raced with the long list of tasks that awaited them over the coming days.

Thirty minutes passed, and she realized she hadn't heard a sound from her father's room. She paused, wiping her hands on a dish towel, thinking he must be so exhausted, emotionally and physically. Deciding to give him more time, she continued to prepare a breakfast fit for a king: pancakes stacked high, crispy bacon, scrambled eggs, and the fresh juice. She even picked a single sunflower from the garden, knowing it had been her mother's favorite. The beautiful yellow flower seemed a small, but significant, tribute to her mother's love for simple beauty.

As the minutes ticked by, Susan grew concerned. Still, no sound came from her father's room. She knocked softly on the door before gently pushing it open, holding the breakfast tray in her hands. What she saw broke her heart. Her father lay in bed, his eyes red and swollen, tears silently streaming down his cheeks. He looked up at her, trying to muster a small, sad smile, but his grief was palpable. She greeted him softly, wishing him a good morning, though it was as far from one as a day could possibly be.

She set the tray on the bedside table and sat beside him, offering the sunflower as a small gesture of warmth and remembrance.

Trying to bring a semblance of normalcy, she said, "Let me help you get up," and reached to pull back the covers. As she did, she noticed the bed was wet.

Her father's face flushed with embarrassment, and he quickly tried to dismiss it. "Oh, sweetie, I don't want you to see this," he murmured, his voice thick with emotion. "Your mother always helped me get out of bed at night to use the restroom. She wasn't here, and I didn't know what to do. Please, don't worry about it. I'll take care of it."

Susan felt a pang of sadness and worry. She hadn't realized the extent of the care her mother had been providing. The thought of her father struggling with such personal needs without her mother's support was heart-wrenching. She helped him to the bathroom, assuring him it was okay, that she was there to help. As he changed into fresh clothes, Susan stripped the bed, her mind racing with concerns. Opening a drawer to find clean sheets, she noticed it was filled with adult diapers. She was staggered by the realization that there were so many things she hadn't known about her father's condition. How long had this been an issue? What else had her mother been quietly managing on her own?

The week that followed was a blur of paperwork, phone calls, and arrangements. Flowers arrived daily, sent by friends and family offering their condolences. The house was filled with the comforting scents of casseroles and baked goods, gifts from church members who dropped by, eager to help in any way they could. It was a time of overwhelming emotions—tears mingled with laughter as they reminisced about happier times, sharing stories of Linda's life and the love she had given so freely. The support from their community was a balm to their grieving hearts, a reminder that they were not alone in their sorrow. Susan's adult children visited their grandfather daily, offering comfort and support. They understood why their mother was spending so much time at his house now, even if just for a short while, to help him adjust to this new, painful reality. Susan's ex-husband also stopped by to pay his respects, bringing a beautiful bouquet of flowers. Susan appreciated this small gesture of kindness in a time of great need.

The funeral came and went, a solemn farewell to a beloved wife and mother. The first week without Linda was a harsh adjustment, followed by the first month. Susan found herself stepping into a new role, increasing her visits to her father's house. Instead of relying on their Sunday church meetings to check in, she made a conscious effort to visit him every other night. She wanted to ensure he was eating well, taking his medications, and that the household was running smoothly. Each visit, she noticed more and more the little things her mother had been doing—small acts of care and love that had kept their home running like a well-oiled machine. The more she discovered, the more concerned she became about her father's ability to manage on his own.

One evening at her women's Bible study, the discussion turned to practical matters, and Susan found herself asking about the new Residential Assisted Living home that had been mentioned before. She inquired if Amy had visited and how it had been for her mother. Amy shared that her mother had moved in and was adjusting well, praising the staff and the homelike environment. Susan listened intently, feeling a mix of relief and apprehension. The idea of her father needing such care felt both inevitable and overwhelming. Determined to explore all options, Susan took down the contact information for the facility and scheduled a visit for the following week. It was a difficult decision, but she knew it was a necessary step to ensure her father received the care he needed. As she prepared for the visit, she prayed for strength and guidance, knowing that whatever the future held, they would walk this path together. This new normal was challenging and uncharted, but she was determined to navigate it with grace and love.

Upon stepping into the Residential Assisted Living home, Susan was immediately enveloped by an unexpected sense of peace and warmth. The air was filled with the delicious, comforting scent of cinnamon bread baking in the oven, evoking memories of cozy family breakfasts. It was a surprising and delightful sensory welcome. As she ventured further inside, the cheerful sounds of laughter reached her ears. Two elderly gentlemen were engrossed in a lively game of checkers, their faces alight with joy and concentration. The rhythmic strumming of a guitar drifted through the room, accompanied by the sweet, nostalgic tunes of oldies music. In another corner, a group of seniors and caregivers danced together, their faces glowing with happiness. The scene was heartwarming and serene, a testament to the vibrant life within these walls. Susan took in the sight of a man napping peacefully in a recliner, a newspaper slipping from his hands, and another resident enjoying a snack at the kitchen table, chatting amiably with a caregiver. It was a bustling, lively environment, yet somehow calm and comforting. It truly felt like a home, not just a facility.

Her eyes then caught sight of Amy's mother, sitting in a cozy armchair by the window. Susan approached her with a warm greeting, noting the woman's contented smile and the way she seemed at ease in this setting. It was a reassuring sight. Susan spent the next hour exploring the home, soaking in the atmosphere and observing the interactions between the residents and staff. She toured an available bedroom, finding it perfectly sized, with a private bathroom and a location near the kitchen and living room, providing easy access to the heart of the home. The tour included discussions with the owner and caregivers, who warmly introduced themselves and explained the daily routines and activities. They detailed the comprehensive care provided, highlighting the personal touches that made this place special. The conversation naturally shifted to costs and logistics. Susan learned that the care her father would need, along with a private room, would be $5,500 per month. It was a significant expense, especially compared to her father's current low cost of living. His mortgage was only $970 a month, with other expenses adding up to about $3,000 total, making this new arrangement a substantial financial leap.

As Susan left the home, she felt an overwhelming sense of comfort. This place wasn't just a facility that claimed to be "homelike" but actually felt like home. The personal, heartfelt care was evident in every interaction she witnessed. The residents seemed genuinely happy, engaged, and well-cared for. Susan was reassured, knowing this environment would provide her father with not only the physical care he needed but also the emotional support and companionship that were crucial as he aged. The idea of him making new friends and being surrounded by round-the-clock care brought her a sense of relief. However, she also felt the weight of the decision ahead, knowing it would be a significant change for her father and an adjustment for both of them.

That evening, Susan visited her father to check on him and ensure he was eating well. As they sat together, she cautiously brought up her visit to the Residential Assisted Living home, carefully describing the spirited atmosphere and the quality of care. She mentioned Amy's mother, highlighting how well she had settled in and the loving community she had found there.

Dennis listened quietly, a slight smile forming on his lips as he absorbed her words. "That's wonderful, sweetie," he said gently, "but I don't need that. I hope you know I'm doing okay." His response was as she had feared—a polite but firm rejection of the idea. Susan was disappointed, but she understood his reluctance. It was hard for anyone to admit they needed more help, especially someone as independent as her father. She knew he took pride in managing on his own and that the idea of leaving his home was daunting.

Internally, Susan grappled with her concerns. She worried about his growing needs and whether she could provide the necessary support alongside the responsibilities of her demanding job. The financial aspect was also daunting, with the cost of the assisted living home being significantly higher than his current expenses. Yet she felt strongly that the peace of mind and quality of life it offered were invaluable. She decided to leave the decision in the hands of the Lord, knowing that this wasn't something to rush. It required time, prayers, and thoughtful conversations. She needed to be patient and understanding, giving her father space to come to terms with the idea. In her heart, she prayed for guidance and wisdom, hoping for clarity on the right path forward. For now, she resolved to continue supporting her father as best she could, visiting him regularly and ensuring his needs were met. She trusted that, in time, the right decision would become clear, and until then, she would hold onto the peace she felt during her visit to the Residential Assisted Living home, believing that it was a place where her father could truly thrive.

Later that month, Susan was busy preparing dinner when her phone rang. Seeing her father's name on the screen, she felt a familiar pang of anxiety. Ever since her mother's passing, her father's calls often carried an undercurrent of worry. Trying to sound cheerful and composed, she answered, "Hi, Daddy!" But her thoughts raced as she awaited his response, her mind already jumping to worst-case scenarios. Dennis's voice on the other end was unsettlingly off. His words were muddled, and he sounded confused.

"Which way should I be turning?" he asked, his voice trembling.

Susan's heart sank, a cold chill running through her. What could he possibly mean by that? Where was he trying to go? Alarm bells went off in her head as she tried to keep calm. "Dad, hold on," she said, her voice steady but urgent. "Let me check my app and see where you are. Is everything okay?"

As she opened the tracking app they had set up on his phone, she heard soft sobs on the other end of the line. Her stomach knotted. The app showed he was just two blocks away from his own home. Relief mixed with concern as she said, "Dad, you're really close. Just park the car and stay where you are. I'm coming to you right now." She quickly grabbed her keys, turned off the stove, and rushed out the door, her thoughts racing.

As she drove the short distance, a myriad of emotions flooded her—worry, fear, and a deep sadness for her father's growing vulnerability. Arriving at the location, she saw his car parked in a quiet neighborhood. He was standing beside it, looking lost and frail under the dimming sky. As she approached, she noticed his shoulders slumped in defeat. She hugged him tightly, feeling his trembling frame.

"What's going on, Dad?" she asked gently, trying to keep her voice calm and reassuring. He sighed deeply, his eyes glistening with unshed tears.

"I went to the grocery store," he explained, his speech full of uncertainty and embarrassment. "It got dark, and I couldn't remember how to get home. I tried to follow the usual streets, but everything looked the same. I circled back to the store three times, but just couldn't figure out the right way. Normally, your mother would help me with directions, but..."

His voice trailed off, the weight of his words hanging heavy in the air. The realization stunned her in this tender, vulnerable moment—this was more than just a temporary lapse; it could be the early signs of something much more serious, like dementia. She didn't know enough about medical conditions to diagnose her father, but she knew this wasn't just a simple mistake. This was a cry for help, whether he realized it or not.

Forcing a reassuring smile, she said, "No problem, Dad. You must have just missed a turn. These streets do all look the same. Follow me and let's get you back home safely."

She guided him back to his car, watching him closely as he settled in. As she led him home, she prayed silently, the moment weighing heavy on her heart. She prayed that her father's mind would be open to the idea of moving to a Residential Assisted Living home, where he could get the care and support he needed.

Once they arrived at the house, she helped him carry in the groceries, chatting lightly to keep the mood as normal as possible. She couldn't shake the image of her father lost and scared, and the realization that he had relied so much on her mother for even the simplest tasks. She stayed with him until he was ready for bed, making sure he was settled and comfortable.

As she tucked him in, she said softly, "I'm glad you called me, Dad. I'm always here to help." He smiled weakly, grateful but still clearly shaken. She kissed his forehead, the familiar gesture filled with a new, deeper meaning. As she left that night, Susan's mind was already preparing for the difficult conversation she knew they needed to have. She would wait until tomorrow to broach the subject, but she knew it couldn't wait much longer. Her father's safety and well-being were at stake. Driving home, she continued to pray for strength, wisdom, and for her father's will to be softened and receptive to the idea.

To her surprise, the next morning, Susan's phone rang early. Seeing her father's name, she answered with a cheerful, "Hey, Pops! What's going on?"

She braced herself for the worst, but instead, Dennis's voice sounded calm and steady. He asked if she wouldn't mind picking him up for church instead of him driving himself. Susan's spirit lifted at this unexpected request, and she eagerly agreed. As they sat through the church service, Susan felt a warmth she hadn't experienced in months. Her father seemed more present and engaged, singing the hymns with a hint of his old vigor. After the service, as they walked back to the car, he suggested they grab sandwiches from the local shop they used to visit after church when she was a child. The suggestion brought a nostalgic smile to her face, and she happily agreed.

They arrived at the quaint sandwich shop, its familiar smell of freshly baked bread and herbs instantly transporting her back to simpler times. They settled into a cozy corner booth—the same one they always chose. As they waited for their food, Dennis looked into Susan's eyes with an intensity she hadn't seen in a while.

Dennis cleared his throat, breaking the silence. "Susan," he began, his voice tender but firm. "You've done so much for me. More than I could ever ask for. You've taken care of everything—probate, the will, the funeral arrangements... You've put your life on hold to help me. But it's not fair to you." He paused, struggling to find the right words. "I know my health is declining. It's been hard without your mother. She did so much for me, things I didn't even realize. And I can't... I don't want to put you in the position of having to take care of me like that. You're my daughter, not my caregiver."

Susan's eyes welled up with tears, a mix of relief and love. She had been praying for this moment, for her father to recognize the reality of their situation. She reached across the table and took his hand, squeezing it gently. "Dad, I love you," she said, her voice choked with emotion. "I'll always be here for you, no matter what. I understand, and I want you to be happy and safe. It's so important to me."

Dennis nodded, his eyes misting over. "I'm open to looking into the home you visited the other day," he continued. "I miss your mother every single day, but I'm getting older. It's not your job to be my caretaker. Can we schedule a visit?"

Susan felt a sudden levity in her body, a sigh of momentary relief lightening the burden she was carrying. This was the answer to her prayers. Joy and gratitude surged within her, a sense of divine intervention. "Hallelujah," she whispered under her breath, unable to contain her happiness. Smiling brightly, she squeezed his hand again. "Of course, Dad. I'll set up a visit for this week. You're going to love it, I promise. And you already know Amy's mom is there, so you'll have a friend right away! The caregivers are amazing, and the owner... she's just the sweetest person." She continued to gush about the home, describing the warm atmosphere, the kind staff, and the engaging community. Dennis listened; a gentle smile danced across his lips.

Following a second tour of Residential Assisted Living home and a heartfelt meet-and-greet with the owner, Susan could tell that Dennis was developing a real sense of belonging, a feeling she knew he had been longing for. After a few more honest and transparent conversations about this new future before him, the decision was made—Sunshine Manor would be his new home. Of course he had concerns, as anyone in the same situation would, but she was patient with him and was relieved when he told her he was ready to give it a try.

Moving in felt like an adventure; at 5,000 square feet, it was the largest and most luxurious home he'd ever lived in. The newness of his surroundings would take some time to get used to, but she knew that the knowledge that he would have his own private bedroom and bathroom would bring him comfort.

From the very first day, Dennis was enveloped in a nurturing environment. The home was staffed with two to three caregivers during the day, and the manager frequently dropped in, ensuring there was always a friendly face available. This unfamiliar abundance of care made Susan and her father feel truly valued. The caregivers didn't just know their responsibilities—they knew the residents, each by name and by heart. They were attuned to the individual needs and histories of the seniors, creating a personalized and loving atmosphere.

Susan visited often, especially in the beginning. Her initial daily visits became a cherished routine for both of them. Whether she stayed for just 30 minutes or spent hours there, the staff always greeted her warmly, offering food and snacks, and encouraging her to stay as long as she wished. The atmosphere was so welcoming that Susan felt as though she was visiting family, not just dropping by a care home. Dennis, though cautious at first, was warming to the idea of sharing the rest of the spacious home with the nine other residents. And it wasn't long before Susan found Dennis engaged in activities with a few other residents. She would see him playing chess with them, his eyes lighting up as he made a clever move. On pet therapy days, he gently petted a rabbit or bunny, a soft smile spreading across his face. The caregivers sometimes organized karaoke sessions, and to Susan's delight, Dennis would join in, singing oldies with surprising enthusiasm. It was as if Sunshine Manor had breathed new life into him; he was more animated and content than she had seen him in years.

The home was just a short 12-minute drive from Susan's house, making spontaneous visits easy and stress-free. The proximity also allowed her to take Dennis out for church services or other activities whenever they wanted, maintaining a sense of normalcy and connection to their community. The caregivers' understanding and compassion extended to talking with Dennis about his late wife. These moments of tenderness that she witnessed between her father and his caregivers brought deep comfort, and she could tell her father relished being seen and understood by people who truly cared about him.

The relief Susan felt was profound. Unlike the guilt that often accompanies the decision to place a loved one in assisted living, Susan felt a deep sense of peace. Sunshine Manor was far from the typical assisted living facility; it was a place of love, care, and community. As time passed, she knew she didn't have to worry about her father; he was in good hands. The anxiety and sleepless nights lessened until they became a distant memory. Instead, she rested easy, confident in the knowledge that her father was thriving.

After spending a month at Sunshine Manor, Dennis began expressing his concerns about the cost of the high-quality care he was receiving. The luxurious and spacious environment, along with the attentive staff must have been expensive. It was a far cry from any home he'd ever owned. He shared his worry that Susan was shouldering too much of a financial burden to keep him there.

One afternoon, as they sat together in the cozy living room of Sunshine Manor, Dennis turned to Susan with gratitude and concern in his eyes. He paused, took a deep breath, and asked her to sell his home and use the proceeds to pay for his care needs. It wasn't an easy request to make, knowing that the money from the sale of his house could have been part of Susan's inheritance. But they both understood that this was a necessary step to ensure he could continue living comfortably and receiving the care he needed.

She had anticipated this conversation, knowing her father well. She assured him that she didn't mind using the funds from the house sale for his care. As a successful career woman, she had built a stable life for herself, even after her divorce. Her children were healthy and happy, and her own home suited her perfectly. While the money from her father's house would have been a nice addition, she had never counted on it to support her lifestyle. Her priority was her father's well-being.

With Susan's help, the sale of Dennis's home went smoothly. Although a bittersweet process, as it marked the finality of a chapter in Dennis's life, Susan knew the money would provide for his needs and bring them both a sense of relief and peace. Dennis told her he was grateful for her being there and guiding him through this transition with compassion and understanding.

Over the next two years, Dennis's experience at Sunshine Manor exceeded all expectations. He blossomed in the supportive environment, making new friends and participating in activities with genuine enjoyment. The staff's kindness and understanding were unwavering, especially during vulnerable moments. Even when Dennis had an accident, the caregivers responded with such compassion that he never felt embarrassed or like a burden. They treated him with dignity and respect, recognizing that aging is a natural part of life.

The highlight of Dennis's time at Sunshine Manor was his 85th birthday celebration. The caregivers and residents came together to throw a party that was nothing short of magical. The decorations, the laughter, and the sense of community made Dennis feel deeply appreciated. It was a day filled with joy, gratitude, and a feeling of being cherished—a dream come true for Dennis and a beautiful affirmation for Susan that they had made the right choice. Sunshine Manor wasn't just a place to live; it was a place where Dennis truly came alive. The love and care he received there made all the difference, not just for him but for Susan as well. The peace of mind she felt, knowing her father was happy and well-cared for, was invaluable. It was a journey of love, trust, and discovery, culminating in a deep, abiding joy for them both.

The proximity of Sunshine Manor to Susan's house was a blessing in so many ways. When Susan adopted a dog the following year, she found joy in taking walks to see her father, bringing the new furry family member along. The casual, homelike atmosphere of Sunshine Manor made these visits feel natural and unforced.

There was no need to navigate a large facility with check-in desks or adhere to strict visiting hours. Susan respected the residents' routines, never visiting too early or too late, but she loved the flexibility to drop by and be part of Dennis's daily life.

As time went on, the close-knit community at Sunshine Manor became even more apparent. The small, intimate setting meant that bonds formed easily among the residents and staff. When Amy's mother passed away, the loss was felt deeply throughout the home. Everyone shared in the sorrow, creating a palpable, somber mood in the house. The caregivers, who had grown attached to the residents, mourned alongside them, showing just how much they cared.

Susan felt the weight of this loss, too. Amy had become a close friend, and Susan empathized with her grief. Amy's prayer request at their Bible study group had initially brought Sunshine Manor to Susan's attention, setting off the chain of events that changed her and Dennis's lives. Now, in the face of loss, Susan found herself drawn especially close to Amy. She helped plan the funeral, offering support and comfort during such a difficult time. They shared a bond that went beyond mere friends; they were both daughters navigating life without their mothers.

This experience underscored the deep sense of community at Sunshine Manor. It wasn't just a place where seniors lived; it was a home where relationships blossomed, and life's joys and sorrows were shared. Their lives were intertwined with the others in this special place, creating a rich tapestry of connection, support, and understanding.

Every holiday season, Susan and her children made Sunshine Manor the epicenter of their family celebrations. They would arrive with an abundance of food, decorations, and an infectious festive spirit, eager to bring joy to the entire community. The house was always beautifully decorated, a testament to the caregivers' dedication, but Susan's family added their own personal touches, especially in Dennis's room. They adorned his space with extra lights, cheerful ornaments, and handmade crafts from the grandchildren, making it a warm and personalized sanctuary.

The holidays were a vibrant mix of singing, dancing, and laughter. The family, along with the seniors and caregivers, celebrated together as one big, extended family. The warmth of these moments was pronounced; the manor filled with the sound of carols and the clink of glasses, the smell of homemade dishes, and the sight of smiles all around. These gatherings were more than just festive events; they were precious moments of connection, joy, and love.

One of the most unforgettable moments came when Susan's first grandchild was born. The family couldn't wait to introduce the newest member to his great-grandfather. They brought the baby to Sunshine Manor, and the sight of Dennis holding his great-grandchild for the first time was a moment that left everyone teary-eyed. The room was filled with laughter and happy tears as they captured these memories in countless photos. It was a milestone that connected generations, a scene that would forever be etched in their hearts.

As Dennis approached his third year at Sunshine Manor, Susan couldn't help but feel a growing sense of concern. She had learned that the average stay in assisted living was only about 3.5 years. The thought of losing her father weighed heavily on her heart, especially since he seemed to be thriving. Every day brought new, delightful stories from the manor. There was a farm animal day where Dennis, beaming with joy, had a sheep nestled in his lap as he sat in his wheelchair. There was also the creative "fishing" day, where residents fished from a tractor bucket filled with real fish—a whimsical activity that brought laughter and excitement. The residents even participated in a gardening project, growing fresh herbs that they later used to cook a delicious dinner together. These experiences were not just activities; they were animated moments of life, filled with engagement and happiness.

One of the surprises for Susan was the stability of the cost of care at Sunshine Manor. While there were occasional increases for improvements like new furniture or upgraded flooring, the overall cost remained relatively steady. This was a pleasant surprise, allowing her to focus more on the quality of life her father enjoyed rather than financial concerns.

Over the years, Susan became the manor's biggest advocate. She recommended the home to everyone she knew who had a senior loved one in need of care. She spoke passionately about the wonderful environment, saying, "Even though my dad's room is so nice, he loves spending time in the living room and the library. He has made friends, and I even stay for dinner sometimes because the food is so delicious!" Her enthusiasm was contagious, and she often found herself singing the praises of the home.

One particularly memorable day was Super Bowl Sunday. Susan had visited her father after church, and she was surprised and delighted to find every senior dressed in either red or white, representing their chosen teams. The caregivers had thoughtfully provided each resident with a jersey, making them feel part of the excitement and camaraderie of the game. It was a small thing, but it meant so much to the residents and their families.

Susan often found herself brimming with gratitude. There were times when she cried tears of joy, touched by the constant communication from the staff, the love and care her father received. She frequently thanked God for leading her to this wonderful place, where her father was so lovingly taken care of. The experience had deepened their relationship, strengthened her bond with her children, and brought her closer to her faith.

The following year, Dennis's health began to decline, a natural consequence of aging. Susan noticed this gradual change and became increasingly concerned about maintaining the quality of his life. She confided in the owner of Sunshine Manor, sharing her deep religious convictions. Susan expressed how challenging it had become to transport her father from the Residential Assisted Living home to their church. She earnestly requested if their pastor could visit Dennis for spiritual guidance and comfort. The owner, understanding the significance of Susan's request, warmly agreed and promptly arranged for the pastor to visit Dennis weekly. They set up a serene and private area in the home where Dennis could meet with the pastor. This gesture filled Susan's heart with gratitude, knowing her father would continue to receive spiritual support.

As Easter approached, Susan received a special invitation from Sunshine Manor for an Easter celebration. She was unaware of the extent of the preparations, but what she witnessed moved her profoundly. The owner had coordinated with a local private Christian school, the same one Susan and her children had attended, to perform their Easter concert for the seniors. Susan was overwhelmed with joy and nostalgia as the children arrived, each carrying a Bible to gift the seniors. The children sang more than half a dozen beautiful songs in a private concert, their voices filling the home with warmth and love. They prayed with the seniors, and listened to their stories, creating a beautiful spiritual connection spanning many generations. The manor staff had invited all the adult children of the residents to the event, making it a memorable and inclusive celebration. To Susan's amazement, three of the guests accepted the Lord into their hearts for the first time that day. Witnessing this transformation sparked a profound sense of purpose within her.

Inspired by the event, Susan felt a calling to do more. She began conversing with the owner of Sunshine Manor about her journey into the assisted living industry. The owner shared her story: years ago, her own mother needed care and assistance, which led her to transition from a real estate investor managing Airbnbs and rental homes to a passionate advocate for senior care. She discovered Residential Assisted Living and decided to take a course at RAL Academy, the nation's premier trainer in the field. Soon after completing the course, she opened Sunshine Manor, her first care home, driven by a mission to provide heartfelt and quality care to seniors.

This story resonated deeply with Susan. An accountant by trade, she had never ventured into real estate beyond her own home, but she had always heard about the potential for great wealth in the industry. More importantly, she now had a newfound passion stirring within her—to help seniors find quality homes in their twilight years.

Determined to follow this path, Susan researched RAL Academy and had a phone call with one of their consultants. Enthusiastic and encouraged, she signed up for an upcoming course and flew to Phoenix, Arizona, to meet the entire RALA team. The experience was transformative. She found herself surrounded by passionate individuals who shared her vision and values. The owner of Sunshine Manor had been right; RAL

Academy was the perfect place to start her journey. Returning home with a renewed sense of purpose, Susan crafted a detailed plan to establish her own Residential Assisted Living home. She was filled with excitement and determination, ready to make a difference in the lives of seniors and their families, just as Sunshine Manor had done for hers.

As time passed, the caregivers at Sunshine Manor began to notice a subtle but profound change in Dennis. They gently informed Susan that her father had started to "talk to Linda" more frequently. With compassion and understanding, they explained that this often happened when someone was nearing the end of their life, preparing to "cross over." Susan, with a heavy heart, understood the implications. She gathered her children and encouraged them to visit their grandpa more often, ensuring they cherished every moment with him. She, too, made a point of spending as much time by his side as possible. During a routine doctor's appointment, the physician gently recommended hospice care for Dennis. This marked a new phase in his journey, one where he would receive additional care and attention from a "visiting angel" who came daily, supplementing the dedicated efforts of the Sunshine Manor caregivers. These visits brought comfort to Dennis and peace of mind to Susan, knowing her father was receiving the utmost care in his final days.

In the weeks that followed, Susan and her children created countless precious memories with Dennis. They laughed, reminisced, and held his hands as they shared stories of the past and dreams for the future. Each visit was a reminder of the deep love that bound them together. Eventually, surrounded by the love of his family and the gentle care of his caregivers, Dennis peacefully passed away. Susan found solace in knowing that he was reunited with Linda and had gone to meet Jesus.

Linda's sudden passing had left Susan heartbroken, with no opportunity for a proper goodbye. The shock and pain of her mother's unexpected death had been a heavy burden, compounded by the responsibility of caring for her father. But Dennis's passing was different. As he took his final breath, Susan felt a rush of peace wash over her, filling her from head to toe. She had done everything in her power to ensure Dennis's comfort and happiness, spending quality time with him and strengthening their bond. She knew without a doubt that Dennis was now in heaven, and the certainty that she would see him again brought her an indescribable sense of calm.

Sunshine Manor had been Dennis's home for nearly four years, a place where he had been cherished and cared for with genuine love. In his memory, the staff planted a sunflower bush in the backyard, a living tribute to his favorite flower. A small plaque was placed beside it, engraved with his favorite Bible verse, serving as a constant reminder of his presence and the joy he brought to those around him.

At Dennis's funeral, the atmosphere was filled with both sorrow and a sense of celebration for a life well-lived. Among the attendees were several caregivers from Sunshine Manor, who had become like extended family over the years. They had grown to love Dennis deeply, sharing countless moments and stories with him. As the service began, one of the caregivers approached Susan, holding a beautifully bound book. "We have something for you," she said softly, handing the memoir to Susan. "We've been working on this with Dennis for some time now."

Susan's eyes welled up with tears as she opened the memoir. Page after page, it was filled with memories of Dennis's life. There were stories of his childhood, growing up with his parents, tales of adventure and mischief. There were tender accounts of how he met Linda, their courtship, and the profound love they shared. Pictures and anecdotes of Dennis as a young father brought back waves of nostalgia, showing him proudly holding his children, teaching them, and sharing moments of joy. The memoir also included details of his favorite hobbies, his likes and dislikes, and even little quirks that made Dennis uniquely him.

As she turned each page, Susan felt a deep sense of connection to her father's life. The caregivers had meticulously gathered these memories, crafting a beautiful tribute that captured the essence of who Dennis was. At the end of the memoir, there was a heartfelt message from the caregivers, thanking Susan for choosing Sunshine Manor. They expressed how, because there were only ten seniors in the care home, they had the time and capacity to truly get to know and love each resident. They thanked Susan for entrusting them with her father's care and shared how much joy and light Dennis had brought into their lives.

Susan was overwhelmed with gratitude. Her appreciation for Sunshine Manor had always been immense, but this gesture deepened her respect and love for the caregivers who had treated her father with such dignity and compassion. She knew that Dennis had been in the best possible place during his final years.

Wanting to give back to the place that had given so much to her and her father, Susan decided against traditional floral tributes. Instead, she placed a QR code on the funeral pamphlet, inviting attendees to make donations to Sunshine Manor. She explained that the home had been a blessing to Dennis and her family, and she wanted to ensure they could continue their wonderful work for other families in need.

As the service concluded and people began to scan the QR code, Susan felt a sense of fulfillment. She knew that her father's legacy would live on not only in the memories of those who loved him but also in the continued support for the care home that had provided him with so much love and comfort. It was a fitting tribute to a man who had lived a life full of love, now helping to provide the same care and compassion to others.

Two years later, Susan realized a dream that had been nurtured by love, loss, and a profound sense of purpose: she opened her own care home, The Sunflower House. The moment one stepped through the front door, it was clear that this was no ordinary assisted living facility. The walls were painted a cheerful, bright yellow, and the home was adorned with radiant flowers, exuding warmth and welcome. Prominently displayed in the entryway was a beautiful photograph of Susan's parents, Dennis and Linda, a tribute to the inspiration behind her journey. The Sunflower House was truly a home filled with love. Susan remained in close contact with the owner of Sunshine Manor, who had become both a mentor and a friend. Some of the caregivers from Sunshine Manor, who had shared the journey with her father, worked part-time at The Sunflower House, bringing with them their compassion and expertise. The shared staff created a sense of continuity and family, ensuring that the care provided was nothing short of exceptional.

The Sunflower House welcomed ten seniors, each one becoming an integral part of the home. Susan poured her heart into providing the best care possible, just as her father had received. Every resident was treated with dignity, respect, and love. Susan quickly realized just how immense the emotional rewards of this work provided. She saw firsthand every little detail of the joy and comfort that quality care brought to both the seniors and their families. What Susan hadn't fully anticipated was the financial success of her venture. By owning and operating The Sunflower House, she was generating a steady cash flow of $15,000 a month. While she hadn't entered the industry for the money, the financial stability was a welcome benefit. The real payoff, however, was the emotional fulfillment she derived from knowing she was making a difference in so many lives.

Eventually, Susan decided to quit her job as an accountant to dedicate herself fully to her passion. Her workweek was structured to allow her to manage the business efficiently while maintaining a personal connection with the home and still having personal freedom of time. Her qualified staff was led by the RAL home manager, her right hand, who oversaw the staff and handled all of the day-to-day responsibilities. Susan spent about five hours a week taking care of administrative tasks and another five hours visiting the home, ensuring everything ran smoothly and hosting tours for prospective residents. Susan particularly enjoyed giving tours of The Sunflower House. She loved hearing the stories of why families were seeking care for their loved ones and how she could help them. Each tour concluded with Susan presenting the family with a sunflower and a heartfelt hug. She prayed over every senior and family that entered the home, making sure they felt confident and comfortable with their decision to trust her with their care.

Susan understood the gravity of her role. With great reward came great responsibility. She was acutely aware that she was being entrusted with the care of someone's most precious asset: their family. This responsibility was never far from her mind. She approached each day with a commitment to honor that trust and provide the best possible care. The Sunflower House wasn't just a business; it was a mission.

Susan had transformed her personal experiences of love, loss, and care into a beacon of hope and comfort for others. The bright yellow walls, the flowers, and the photos of her parents weren't just decorations—they were symbols of the love and dedication that defined The Sunflower House. And in every corner of the home, from the cozy common areas to the peaceful private rooms, that love was palpable.

Susan's story is one of loss and joy, ultimately culminating in a profound sense of gratitude and fulfillment. She remains immensely thankful for the decision to place her father in a Residential Assisted Living home. For nearly four years, Dennis received exceptional care from people who truly loved and understood him. The caregivers at Sunshine Manor didn't just perform their duties; they genuinely made an effort to be by Dennis's side, offering companionship and compassion during the hardships of aging.

For Susan, Sunshine Manor was not just a place that resembled home—it was home. It was not just family-like; it was family. Although losing her father was a deeply sorrowful experience, she found solace in knowing that he had spent his final years surrounded by love and exceptional care. There were no regrets, only the certainty that placing Dennis in an RAL home had been the best decision she could have made.

Her children, too, were grateful for the extended time they had with their grandpa, and her youngest ones cherished the moments with their great-grandpa. These precious interactions would not have been possible without the supportive environment of Sunshine Manor. The relationships Susan built with the owner, operators, and caregivers became invaluable, forging bonds she never anticipated. This experience transformed Susan's life, igniting a passion for Residential Assisted Living. She became a staunch advocate for RAL homes, recognizing their immense value. Carrying forward the RAL Academy's message of "doing good and doing well," Susan dedicated herself to every family she met. She understood the profound trust placed in her hands and made it her mission to honor that trust by providing the same level of love and care she had witnessed at Sunshine Manor. Through her work, Susan continues to impact lives, ensuring that every senior in her care feels beloved and every family feels supported. Her journey, born out of love for her father, has become a guiding light, bringing hope and comfort to many others, reflecting the true spirit of Residential Assisted Living.

KEY TAKEAWAYS

Susan's story is a beautiful example of how the journey in Residential Assisted Living can be a blessing, both to seniors and their loving family members. Susan recognized her limited capacity to handle the growing needs of her aging father. She sought the help of others and didn't quit until she found the right place for her father, a place where he could spend his twilight years surrounded by the love and support that he deserved.

The unvarnished reality is that far too few seniors end up with this kind of story. Oftentimes, it comes down to simply not knowing that there are alternatives to the nursing home industry that has been pervasive in America for decades. As a nation, we are slowly coming to terms with the fact that the way we have cared for our elderly simply isn't adequate. We have a long way to go, but we are making strides. And it starts with informing the people that there is a better way. We can do better. Our seniors deserve better. In fact, there are a lot of commonly held beliefs around aging seniors that need to be addressed if we want to make real change in this industry.

CHAPTER 6:
CLEARING THE AIR

*"Addressing misunderstandings that
have long plagued the industry"*

Elder care is a critical and sensitive topic that touches the lives of nearly every family. As our population ages, more and more families are facing decisions about how to provide the best care for their elderly loved ones. Unfortunately, this field is rife with misconceptions that can cloud judgment and lead to poor decisions resulting in inadequate care. It's crucial to challenge these myths with facts and insights to ensure that better choices can be made to help more seniors receive the care and respect they deserve.

Here are some of the most common misconceptions people have about elder care today:

MYTH 1: SENIORS LOSE INTEREST IN THE WORLD AROUND THEM

The stereotype of disinterested, disengaged seniors couldn't be further from the truth. Many seniors are incredibly engaged with life, maintaining a keen interest in world events, pursuing hobbies, and enjoying social activities. Many even have a zest for life that rivals that of younger generations, seeking out new experiences, nurturing relationships, and contributing to their communities in meaningful ways. Seniors may not always appear to want to engage in community around them, but it might just be that they don't fully understand how they can. Fitting into this fast-paced society that continues to evolve in ways that none of us can predict might seem daunting to those who have known a slower, more predictable existence their whole lives. But that doesn't mean they don't want to participate or that they don't have anything to offer the generations that come after them. The sheer volume of stories, lessons learned and life experiences that our seniors hold within them is truly one of our most precious and untapped resources.

MYTH 2: MENTAL AND PHYSICAL DECLINE IS INEVITABLE

While it's true that aging can bring about changes in both mental and physical capacities, the notion that all seniors will experience severe decline is a gross exaggeration. This belief is not only misleading but can also be detrimental to the perception and treatment of the elderly in society. The extent and severity of mental and physical changes with aging vary widely among individuals. Many seniors lead remarkably active lives, remain mentally sharp, and are more than capable of learning new skills and adapting to new technologies. The key to supporting our aging population lies in recognizing and nurturing their potential. This involves providing resources, opportunities, and environments that are attuned to their unique abilities and interests. By doing so, we can help seniors maintain their independence and quality of life.

MYTH 3: ELDER CARE FACILITIES ARE DEPRESSING AND LIFELESS

The image of all elder care facilities being grim and joyless places is outdated and inaccurate. Today, many senior care facilities are shedding the old stigma and are now recognized for their vibrant atmospheres, where the focus is on living a full and joyful life. Senior living, especially the smaller, boutique-style Residential Assisted Living homes, is nothing like the sterile, institutional settings that many may still envision. They are now designed with the residents' well-being in mind, offering a variety of activities that cater to both the physical and mental health of the individuals. From art classes and music therapy to gardening clubs and special event celebrations, these facilities provide a plethora of options to keep the residents actively engaged and form meaningful connections with their peers. The staff at these homes are also trained to provide not just medical support, but also emotional and psychological assistance. Qualified staff work tirelessly to create an environment that is not only safe and secure, but also warm and inviting. The goal is to make these facilities feel like home, where residents can enjoy their golden years with dignity and respect.

MYTH 4: OLDER ADULTS DON'T NEED OR WANT CLOSE RELATIONSHIPS

Humans are inherently social creatures, and this aspect of our nature does not simply fade away with age. On the contrary, many seniors place a high value on their relationships. They understand the importance of social interaction and its positive impact on their mental and emotional health, and many will often go to great lengths to maintain and forge new connections. Companionship and emotional bonds are crucial for well-being, and many seniors find great joy and comfort in their relationships with family, friends, and caregivers.

The desire for connection can manifest in various ways among older adults. Many find solace and happiness in the company of family, cherishing the time spent with children and grandchildren. These intergenerational interactions can provide seniors with a sense of continuity and belonging, as well as opportunities to impart wisdom and share experiences. Friendships, too, play a vital role in the lives of seniors. Long-standing friendships often provide a source of comfort and stability, while new friendships can invigorate and bring fresh perspectives into their lives. Social activities, community groups, and hobby clubs are just a few avenues through which seniors can connect with peers who share similar interests. Caregivers and RAL staff can also form an essential part of the social fabric for many older adults. The relationship between a senior and their caregiver can go beyond the provision of basic needs, evolving into a meaningful and mutually rewarding bond. Caregivers can become trusted confidants and a key component of the senior's support system.

It is crucial to acknowledge the efforts seniors make to preserve and establish these connections. Recognizing and supporting the social needs of seniors is fundamental to promoting their overall health, and it's a reminder that the human need for connection transcends age and remains a vital part of life at every stage.

MYTH 5: ELDER CARE IS ONLY FOR THOSE WHO ARE ILL

Elder care services encompass a broad spectrum of support, extending far beyond the needs of the ill. Sure, they are designed to assist those who may require help with daily living activities, but they are also beneficial for those who simply wish to live in a more community-focused setting. Senior care services are not just about providing medical assistance; they are about enhancing the overall quality of life for seniors. In addition to helping with everyday tasks such as bathing, dressing, and eating, which can become challenging as one ages, they also include social engagement activities, transportation, and even financial management assistance, all of which contribute to a senior's independence and well-being.

Living in a community setting can be particularly beneficial for seniors who are looking for companionship and social interaction. These communities often provide a variety of programs, like educational classes, exercise sessions, and specialty events, all of which encourage seniors to stay active and engaged. The benefits in these communities offer a sense of security and peace of mind, not only for the seniors themselves but also for their families. Depending on the care facility, services can be tailored to fit the individual needs of each senior, ensuring that they receive the level of support that is just right for them. This is one of the many areas where smaller Residential Assisted Living homes really shine. A more personalized approach helps seniors maintain their independence for as long as possible, promoting a sense of dignity and self-worth.

MYTH 6: CAREGIVERS ARE UNTRAINED AND UNSKILLED

The notion that caregivers in the senior living industry are all untrained and unskilled is a misconception and, depending on the senior facility, often couldn't be further from the truth. Caregiving is a role that requires a diverse and comprehensive skillset, blending both technical knowledge and soft skills to cater to the complex needs of the elderly.

Caregivers are often the unsung heroes in the healthcare sector, undergoing extensive training programs that equip them with the necessary medical procedures, emergency response capabilities, and an understanding of the intricacies involved in personal care. These training programs are rigorous and designed to prepare caregivers for a wide range of scenarios they might encounter while providing care.

Beyond initial training, many caregivers continue to enhance their expertise through certifications and ongoing education, particularly in specialized areas of care such as managing dementia or providing palliative support. This commitment to continuous learning demonstrates their dedication to the profession and their desire to provide the highest quality of care. Furthermore, caregivers often bring a level of compassion and commitment that goes far beyond their technical abilities. Passionate caregivers understand the importance of creating a nurturing environment for the elderly, often forming close bonds with those they care for and becoming an integral part of their lives. Their role is not just about health management; it's about enriching the lives of the elderly with dignity and respect.

Are there some caregivers out there who are bad eggs? Sure. Just like in any other profession. But for many, caregiving is not merely a job—it's a calling that attracts dedicated individuals who are committed to making a positive impact in the lives of seniors. These people are skilled professionals who ensure the comfort and safety of the elderly, often going above and beyond the call of duty to provide care that is both compassionate and competent. It's time to recognize and appreciate the invaluable service these individuals provide to the most vulnerable in our society.

MYTH 7: ELDER CARE OPTIONS ARE LIMITED

One of the most prevalent misconceptions surrounding elder care is the belief that options for senior care are scarce and homogenous. This misconception often stems from a lack of information and understanding about the wide array of services available to support the aging population. The truth is the elder care industry has evolved significantly, offering a comprehensive range of services that cater to the diverse and changing needs of seniors.

In-home care services, for instance, provide seniors with the necessary assistance to manage their daily activities while allowing them to remain in the comfort of their own homes. These services can range from basic help with chores and errands to more involved personal care and medical assistance.

Adult day care centers serve as another option, especially for families that have the freedom and ability to care for their own aging loved ones, but need daytime support and a break from the round-the-clock care they provide. These centers offer a safe and stimulating environment where seniors can participate in various activities, receive meals, and access health services.

Assisted living communities present a unique blend of independence and support, where seniors can enjoy their own space with the added benefit of available care and social activities. These communities, especially Residential Assisted Living homes, are designed to foster a sense of belonging and provide opportunities for engagement and interaction among residents. Like the story of Susan and her father, Residential Assisted Living offers a plethora of unique benefits, both to the senior and their family, ensuring that seniors spend their twilight years surrounded by love, comfort, and appropriate personal care.

Each senior care solution is tailored to provide different levels of support, which is why it's important to find the most appropriate environment based on the individual needs of the senior. The overall goal is to enhance the quality of life, regardless of the care setting chosen. By understanding the full scope of options available, families can make informed decisions that align with their loved ones' desires and requirements, ultimately leading to better outcomes for all involved. It's crucial to recognize that elder care is not a one-size-fits-all service, but rather a multifaceted field dedicated to accommodating the unique journey of each senior.

MYTH 8: ELDER CARE IS ALWAYS EXTREMELY EXPENSIVE

The cost of elder care is often a significant concern. The assumption that it is always extremely expensive can cause unnecessary anxiety and stress for families. The landscape of elder care is diverse, and so too are the costs associated with it. While it's true that some care options can be quite costly, there is a wide range of financial assistance programs available to help manage these expenses. A variety of government programs, such as Medicare and Medicaid, are designed to alleviate some of the financial burdens. These programs can cover a range of services from in-home care to skilled nursing facilities. However, eligibility criteria and the extent of coverage can vary, making it imperative for individuals and families to explore these options thoroughly.

In addition to government assistance, numerous nonprofit organizations are dedicated to supporting seniors and their families as they navigate the costs of care. These organizations often provide resources, counseling, and sometimes direct financial assistance, helping to bridge the gap between what is needed and what can be afforded. Insurance plans also play a critical role in managing elder care expenses. Long-term care insurance, in particular, is designed to cover services that traditional health insurance plans may not, such as assistance with daily living activities and extended nursing home stays. Understanding the intricacies of these insurance policies and how they integrate with other forms of assistance is crucial.

Furthermore, many elder care facilities and service providers recognize the financial challenges faced by families and offer scalable services. This means that the level of care and support can be adjusted according to individual needs and financial capabilities, ensuring that quality care remains within reach for a wider range of people.

It's important to note that the cost of elder care is not solely a financial matter; it's also about value. Investing in senior care is investing in the quality of life and well-being of the senior. By conducting comprehensive research, consulting with advisors, and engaging with senior living professionals, families can gain a clearer understanding of the resources available to them. This knowledge empowers families to make informed decisions. The key is to approach senior care with a strategy that encompasses all available resources, ensuring that the care provided is both affordable and adequate for the individual's needs.

By understanding the realities of elder care, we can approach the topic with a more informed and compassionate perspective. It's essential to research, ask questions, and seek out reliable sources to uncover the truth behind these misconceptions. With the right knowledge, we can make better decisions for the care of our elderly loved ones and ensure they live their later years with dignity and joy.

It's time to embrace a more accurate and respectful perspective on senior care; one that acknowledges the vitality, contributions, needs, desires, and significance of our older adults. By advocating for quality elder care, and building a society that values and supports its senior members, together, we can create a brighter future for our elderly loved ones.

CHAPTER 7

THE CUSP OF A REVOLUTION

*"A roadmap to continue the journey
of compassionate care"*

The inspiration to write this book comes from the countless stories we hear about families enduring horrific experiences and/or harboring misconceptions regarding the nature of assisted living. Each story, whether it's from a distressed family member or a concerned caregiver, reinforces our resolve to set the record straight and provide hope and clarity in the often murky waters of senior housing.

We aim to dispel the myths surrounding senior care and illuminate the best choices available to families. There are numerous RAL homes across the country that operate with the highest standards, prioritizing the health and well-being of their residents above all. These homes are sanctuaries where seniors receive the respect, care, and dignity they deserve. However, they often go unnoticed, overshadowed by the more prominent, commercialized facilities with larger marketing budgets. Our mission is to bring these exemplary RAL homes into the spotlight and provide families with the guidance and resources to find them more easily.

It is so important to educate yourself on what is available to you in your area. Many of these smaller, more personalized Residential Assisted Living homes go relatively unnoticed because their owners are more focused on care than marketing, and they usually thrive by word of mouth anyway. Unless someone has had personal exposure to these types of homes, or know someone who has, they may not even realize they exist. Our goal is to change that, to make Residential Assisted Living a well-known and respected option in the senior living sector.

The aging baby boomer generation is casting a new light on our industry. As the demand for senior living increases, the attention on quality RAL homes grows, leading to more positive outcomes for seniors and their families. This shift is long overdue. For generations, the default option for many families was to send their elderly loved ones to cold, sterile, hospital-like nursing homes, where they quickly became just another number. Thankfully, the public is gradually realizing that the glossy exteriors and lofty promises of many large, commercialized assisted living options often fall short of delivering genuine care and compassion.

We are on the cusp of a revolution in senior care. Residential Assisted Living homes, with their focus on personalized care and community, are emerging as a shining example to the industry that there is a better way. This book is our effort to help accelerate that change, to guide families toward better choices, and to celebrate the homes that are setting the gold standard in senior living. By sharing these stories and insights, we hope to inspire a widespread recognition and appreciation for the incredible work being done in RAL homes across the country.

This journey is not just about correcting misconceptions; it's about transforming lives. It's about ensuring that every senior can spend their later years in a place where they feel safe, cherished, and truly at home. And it's about empowering families with the knowledge and tools to make informed decisions that honor and respect their loved ones. This is our passion and our mission.

More and more evidence is surfacing about the deficiencies often found in larger senior living establishments. Real people with real stories of horrible experiences with the big-box facilities are challenging the status quo in senior housing. Subpar food quality, high staff-to-resident ratios, and inadequate care are just a few of the issues regularly brought to light. As these stories circulate, families and prospective senior living residents are increasingly voting with their dollars, seeking out the benefits of smaller, more intimate, homelike settings found in Residential Assisted Living. This growing awareness is prompting a crucial shift. People are starting to ask, "What else is out there?" They are driven by the conviction that there must be safer and more fulfilling options available for their aging loved ones. This search for alternatives is not just a trend; it's a movement fueled by a deep desire to find dignified, loving care.

The COVID-19 pandemic was a significant obstacle for the senior housing industry, but it also provided an unexpected opportunity for Residential Assisted Living homes to shine. As large, impersonal facilities struggled with outbreaks and isolation, the true value of smaller, more personal care homes became evident. Families, disillusioned by the lack of care and quality in big-box facilities, began to seek out RAL homes, desperate to find a better environment for their loved ones. This exposure was a step in the right direction, but there's still so much more to do.

In today's uncertain economic climate, investing in something with heart and genuine care has become increasingly important. Money cannot be the driver of decision-making, or it will show through eventually; it must be about the well-being of our loved ones. Unfortunately, with the rising costs of living, many families find themselves without the budget to afford exorbitantly priced facilities. This financial strain often leads to poor decisions followed by guilt.

Resorting to in-home care might seem like a good option initially, but as we explored earlier, it can place an immense strain on families, and still end up falling short in terms of quality. The familiar surroundings, the comfort of home, and the idea of providing personalized care all start with good intentions. However, the resentment and anger that can arise among siblings, the stress of providing constant care, and the challenging dynamics that emerge when a parent is in an undignified position can be overwhelming. The parent you once loved and respected can become someone you hardly recognize, shaking you to your core. Residential Assisted Living homes offer a solution to these challenges. They provide a nurturing environment where seniors can maintain their dignity and families can find peace of mind. This type of care helps to preserve the familial relationships that can so easily become strained under the weight of home caregiving.

We explain these negatives often found in large facilities and in-home care with a caveat. There are some families that have wonderful experiences with larger facilities. They find the assistance and care their elderly loved one needs, and there is no resentment or anger toward the situation. The financial burden is manageable, and their loved one passes peacefully in a setting that feels just right for everyone involved.

And there are some families who choose to keep their loved ones at home and experience beautiful outcomes. They grow closer, their communication improves, and they treasure the additional time spent together. The senior enjoys precious moments with younger generations, moments that might not have been possible otherwise. This arrangement can save time and money, transforming what might have been a challenging situation into a profound blessing.

We don't want anyone reading this to think that Residential Assisted Living is the only good option. Every family has different wants and needs, and it's vital that you take time to sit down and think about what's best for you and your family at the moment. Senior housing decisions can feel like choosing an avocado: it's often not on your mind until suddenly, it's urgent. It isn't ripe for a long time, then it's perfect for three days, and then it's overripe shortly after. Before you need senior housing, you don't worry about it much. It probably rarely comes to mind. It's almost something you feel you could push off thinking about because it seems so out of reach. But then all of the sudden… you need it… and you need it NOW! You might find yourself needing to make a decision quickly, sometimes within days or even hours.

The urgency of such an important decision highlights the need for proactive planning. Senior housing decisions impact the well-being and quality of life of someone you love deeply. These decisions should not be rushed. Take the time to explore all of your options, do thorough research, and understand the places you want to avoid as well as those that might be a perfect fit for your family. Discuss financial obligations openly with your senior loved ones and other family members involved. Remember, there is no one-size-fits-all solution. Each family's situation is unique, and what works for one may not work for another.

For those considering an RAL home, you can find the entire updated lists of RAL homes across the US at www.RALHomeLocator.com. Or you can search your state's Department of Human Services (DHS) website. If you use the DHS website, just be sure to sort through the listings to determine which are small group homes, as opposed to the large, big-box facilities, because the categories may not be clearly sorted for you. You will want to look for homes with 6 to 16 beds located in residential neighborhoods.

Ultimately, the key is to be informed and prepared. Whether you choose a large facility, in-home care, or a Residential Assisted Living home, the goal is to ensure your loved one receives the care, respect, and the dignity they deserve. This decision is about their life and your peace of mind. Make the choice with care, consideration, and the knowledge that you are doing what's best for your family's unique situation.

CHAPTER 8

EMPOWERING ALL TO PURSUE QUALITY CARE

*"Inspiring a new generation to challenge the
status quo and innovate with heart"*

If you're considering starting your own care home, we at the Residential Assisted Living Academy are here to guide and train you every step of the way. Over the past decade, we've helped thousands of individuals across all 50 states create thriving, compassionate Residential Assisted Living homes. Our success stories span the nation, demonstrating the profound impact that dedicated care can have on seniors and their families. Whether you're a medical professional, a real estate expert, or just someone interested in expanding your portfolio, this could be an incredible opportunity for you. However, your profession doesn't matter as much as your heart and passion. Anyone who genuinely cares for seniors and wants to make a difference is welcomed with open arms. Imagine the possibility: your loved one could live for free in your own Residential Assisted Living home, while you generate income from the business. It could be the perfect solution to a current challenge or a proactive step for future needs.

At the Residential Assisted Living Academy, our mission is to positively impact 10 million seniors through Residential Assisted Living. But we can't do it alone. We need compassionate, dedicated individuals like you to open care homes and help transform the industry. The traditional big-box facilities don't have to be the only option. You don't have to sacrifice your life to care for your aging parents or loved ones. There is a better way, and it's a solution that benefits everyone involved. Our training equips you with the knowledge and skills needed to create a nurturing, homelike environment for seniors. You'll learn how to provide high-quality care, manage the day-to-day operations, and ensure the financial viability of your home. More importantly, you'll become part of a movement that is redefining senior care for the better.

Imagine a world where seniors are treated with the respect, love, and dignity they deserve, in a setting that feels like home. This is the vision we're working towards, and we invite you to join us. By starting your own Residential Assisted Living home, you'll be providing an invaluable service to your community and offering a compassionate alternative to the often impersonal care found in larger facilities. Our training program covers everything you need to know, from regulatory requirements to marketing strategies, ensuring you're fully prepared to succeed. We offer ongoing support and a network of like-minded individuals who share a passion for senior care. Together, we can make a significant difference in the lives of millions of seniors and their families. Don't let the challenges of senior care overwhelm you. With the right training and support, you can create a loving, supportive environment that benefits everyone involved. Join us at the Residential Assisted Living Academy and become part of a movement that is changing the face of senior care. We promise you'll find it to be one of the most rewarding decisions you'll ever make.

The need for quality RAL homes is only growing. Consider the facts: 4,000 people turn 65 every day, and 10,000 people turn 85 every day. While 90 percent of people wish to stay in their own homes, 70 percent will need daily care for an average of three years. The silver tsunami of seniors is coming, and it's essential to understand and consider the options available before you're overwhelmed by the wave.

Above all else, if a small care home is trying to open in your community, please don't be one of those "not in my backyard" neighbors, trying to shut them down or make opening their care home a huge struggle. These homes are not trying to ruin your neighborhood, nor are they trying to bring excessive traffic, ambulances, or disruption to your streets. Instead, they are striving to bring meaningful solutions and compassionate care to your community. Take the time to talk with the new owners and understand their vision. See how you can support them on their journey. This industry requires individuals with big hearts who are committed to following rules and regulations meticulously. But just as crucial as their dedication is the support they receive from their community. Be a leader. Even if the RAL home opening down the street isn't your own, support those who are embarking on this noble venture. Stand with them, not against them. Trust me, this is not an Airbnb with late-night parties. This is a beautiful, quiet home filled with lovely seniors who need assistance at the end of their lives. By welcoming and supporting RAL homes in your neighborhood, you are contributing to a much-needed solution. This is not just about providing a place to live; it's about creating a space where seniors can thrive. Imagine the impact on your community: a serene, respectful environment where seniors are cherished and cared for, where families find relief knowing their loved ones are in good hands.

We all have a role to play in shaping the future of senior care. By supporting RAL homes, you are not only helping your neighbors who are opening these homes, but also contributing to a broader movement that seeks to improve the quality of life for seniors everywhere. It's about building a community that values and respects its elderly members. So, the next time a small care home tries to open in your neighborhood, choose to be a supporter. Extend a hand, offer your help, and show your solidarity. This industry thrives on community support, and your positive attitude can make a significant difference. You may find that by supporting a local RAL home, you're not only helping others but also paving the way for options that might benefit your own family in the future. The silver tsunami is coming, and we need to be prepared. It's true that a single thoughtful individual can't change the world alone, but together, as a community, we can create a profound impact. Let's work together to ensure that our seniors receive the care, love, and respect they deserve. To learn more about the RAL Academy, please visit <u>RALAcademy.com</u>.

Do Good and Do Well.

QUESTIONS TO ASK FAMILY MEMBERS ABOUT SENIOR CARE NEEDS

Approaching these questions with empathy and respect can help facilitate a collaborative and informed decision-making process within a family. We highly recommend going through these 40 questions with all pertinent parties, ensuring all options are discussed and all voices and opinions are heard.

1. What are our loved one's current care needs?
2. What needs do we anticipate becoming more significant over time?
3. Which activities of daily living do our loved one find challenging?
4. Are there any specific health concerns or chronic conditions that might require special attention in the future?
5. How effectively are they managing their medications?
6. How is their memory?

7. How is their emotional well-being?

8. Are they lonely or isolated at home?

9. Do they need assistance with personal care tasks (e.g., bathing, dressing, grooming, etc.)?

10. Are they able to manage mobility challenges independently?

11. What physical support can family members provide comfortably?

12. What financial support can family members provide comfortably?

13. Does our loved one have a plan to pay for their care needs?

14. Have they chosen a specific home, institution, or facility for future care?

15. Is aging in place a realistic option for our senior loved one?

16. What home modifications are needed to ensure their safety and comfort until the end?

17. Would they require additional oversight if they chose to stay at home?

18. Are there community resources available to support aging in place?

19. What is our budget for their assisted living needs?

20. How long can we sustain this budget?

21. Do we need an agreement among siblings/partners for payment schedules and amounts?

22. Do we need an agreement among siblings/partners for visitation or communication schedules with our elderly loved one?

23. How will we communicate about changes in our loved one's needs?

24. Who will take the lead on decision-making, and is everyone comfortable with this choice?

25. How important is proximity to our senior loved one?
26. What amenities and services are important to our elderly loved one?
27. How does our senior loved one feel about moving out of their home and into a new setting?
28. Who will lead the conversation with our senior loved one about these decisions?
29. What emotional support can family members provide during the transition?
30. What visitation schedule will family members agree upon?
31. How flexible is the chosen assisted living home or facility in accommodating changing needs for care?
32. What provisions are in place for more advanced care if necessary in the future?
33. Are there any additional costs we can expect due to changing needs or time spent in the home/facility?
34. What is the resident-to-caregiver ratio in the home/facility?
35. How important are cost, location, and amenities?
36. How will the transition impact family dynamics?
37. Who will be responsible for the estate and financial decisions outside of assisted living (e.g., savings, investments, insurance, properties, belongings, etc.)?
38. Do we know anyone who has had a positive experience in an assisted living facility near the location we are considering?
39. Who will be responsible for researching facility or home options, including reviews, testimonials, and tours?
40. What is everyone's top priority or desired outcome?

ABOUT THE AUTHORS

ISABELLE GUARINO is one of the foremost authorities in the field of Residential Assisted Living, with over a decade of experience in senior housing, real estate, and business. As the COO of the Residential Assisted Living Academy, she has dedicated her career to educating and empowering individuals motivated to create quality care environments for seniors.

With a background that blends business development and a passion for helping others, Isabelle, along with her family, recognized the growing need for residential alternatives to traditional nursing homes. Her father, Gene Guarino, the "Godfather of Residential Assisted Living," had a vision to establish the RAL Academy, which provides comprehensive training, resources, and support for aspiring assisted living operators. Under her leadership, the RAL Academy has become the premiere institution for those looking to enter the field, with a focus not only on operational excellence but also on fostering empathy and the highest-quality care for residents. She works tirelessly to equip aspiring RAL owners and caregivers with the knowledge and skills necessary to succeed in this rewarding field.

Isabelle is also a sought-after speaker, author, and consultant, frequently sharing her insights at industry conferences and workshops. Her expertise spans a wide array of topics, from regulatory compliance and business development to effective resident engagement and marketing strategies. Isabelle's passion for advocacy has led her to collaborate with top organizations focused on improving standards in senior care. She is dedicated to promoting a culture of care that honors the dignity and individuality of every resident, believing that everyone deserves a safe and nurturing environment in their golden years.

KURT COLEMAN is a writer and editor for the Residential Assisted Living Academy, and has dedicated nearly a decade to researching every facet of the senior housing industry. He brings a wealth of knowledge to an industry that for many can often seem confusing or overwhelming. Kurt is focused on creating and enhancing resources that help RAL owners and care workers improve their assisted living businesses, as well as providing the families of seniors with the information they need to find the best care home for aging loved ones.

Through this book, Isabelle and Kurt aim to share their extensive knowledge and practical insights, empowering and motivating readers to go out and build vibrant, supportive communities that enhance the lives of seniors and their families.

To learn more about Residential Assisted Living
and how you can get involved, head to:

RALAcademy.com

Or check out our other books, *Living Legacy, Silver Tsunami,* or the *Investor's Guide to Senior Housing.*